Anonymous

The Valley of Wyoming

The Romance of its History and its Poetry

Anonymous

The Valley of Wyoming
The Romance of its History and its Poetry

ISBN/EAN: 9783337348601

Printed in Europe, USA, Canada, Australia, Japan

Cover: Foto ©Andreas Hilbeck / pixelio.de

More available books at **www.hansebooks.com**

THE

VALLEY OF WYOMING:

THE ROMANCE

OF ITS

HISTORY AND ITS POETRY.

ALSO,

SPECIMENS OF INDIAN ELOQUENCE.

COMPILED BY A

NATIVE OF THE VALLEY.

NEW YORK:

ROBT. H. JOHNSTON & CO.:

AND SOLD BY

C. E. BUTLER, WILKES-BARRE, PA.

1866.

CONTENTS.

PREFATORY NOTE.

THE Summer tourist, or the traveller from foreign lands, often finds himself embarrassed by the great variety and exquisite beauty of American scenery. In such a moment of doubt, let him decide in favor of that matchless valley declared by Colonel Stone to be superior in its real charms even to Dr. Johnson's ideal of the Happy Valley of Amhara, which he describes as the perfection of an earthly abode.

The decision being made, the traveller has looked in vain for a little hand-book to serve as an intelligent guide to the natural curiosities and beauties, bloody fields and antiquities, of Wyoming. He could hardly find a separate copy of Campbell's imaginative and exquisite poem. He was fain either to supply himself with the voluminous and exhaustive pages of Miner, and similar works, or he must trust himself to the disjointed and sometimes rhapsodized legends of the cicerones of the valley.

This little volume, which has not the slightest claim to be either a history or a study of romance, is presented as just such a hand-book as the tourist will need. The visitor to Wyoming will find it a guide to his feet, and the visitors of former years may in its pages renew the charming itinerary at their own firesides.

In the extracts here presented may be found the true romance of the history of Wyoming, most romantic because simply true.

The brief compilation given will serve to interest the visitor, and the slight sketch of men and events will need no very vivid imagination to reproduce for him the figures of the early colonists, to conjure up the desperate conflicts, the Indian war-whoop, the shrieking women and children, the smoking desolation.

The great poem of Campbell has been appended; for although it is not entirely true to external nature, it is most delicately true to human nature, and appeals directly to the human heart. It, more than veritable history, has made known the sad story of Wyoming wherever the English language is read; and it will perpetuate that story where histories are unknown, and when histories shall be forgotten. " Oh, happy privilege of genius," says Leigh Hunt, in speaking of Priam before Achilles, " that can reach out its hand from a thousand years back, and touch our eyelids with tears !"

It is worthy to be remembered in passing, that the beauty of " Susquehanna's side," as depicted by Campbell, gave to the great Lakers their idea of selecting it as a spot upon which to try their wild scheme of Pantisocracy at the beginning of this century, a scheme abandoned while in embryo.

Nor is this the only poetic garland hung among the wild flowers on her ruined wall. Our own Halleck, dreaming in the happy valley, one day wakened into sudden song, declaring, as he gazed :—

> " Nature hath made thee lovelier than the power
> Even of Campbell's pen hath pictured."

A few other poems, chiefly of local and antiquarian value, have been added for the tourist's behoof, and he may thus move among the Wyoming people to the songs of their own making.

NEW YORK, 1866.

INTRODUCTORY.

WYOMING! who has not heard the name of the beautiful valley through which the Susquehanna glides, " fair Wyoming," with her mountain walks, her story-telling glens, her founts and brooks, and maids as dew-drops pure and fair, which the soul with grandeur fill, and melody and love?

Who has not heard, too, her sad story? It has been elaborated by the pen of the historian, and immortalized in the lofty rhyme of the poet. Wyoming! thine, indeed, was the fatal gift of beauty, that dowry which is so often fraught with woe to its inheritor. For its possession and enjoyment contending tribes of the red men fought; and when wrenched from their grasp by force, or fraud, or treachery, and white men, bearing the casket of a better civilization, had come within her borders, and she had received the baptism of blood as a seal, even then followed contentions, and tumults, and bloody wars between factions of the pale faces: the issue was to decide which should have her to hold and to enjoy. It is not to be wondered at that the poor Indian, untaught, selfish by intuition, and believing in the law of might, should have fought long and well to retain the possession of that which to him was a terrestrial paradise.

There were no nobler hunting-grounds, nor a more beautiful wigwam-home. Nature was lavish of supply, and prodigal of health and happiness.

Here was the mountain, the plain, and the river, each of its kind the noblest ; the mountain for hunting, the river for fishing, and the plain for planting. But why, after its possession by the white man had been secured, brothers with brothers should contend, it is not designed in this compilation fully to explain. A few brief facts we shall give, and let our readers gather the philosophy for themselves.* It is the old paradox of pundit and poet :—

> " Strange—that where nature loved to trace,
>   As if for gods a dwelling-place,
>   And every charm and grace had mixed
>   Within the paradise she fixed,
>   There man, enamored of distress,
>   Should mar it into wilderness."

---

* For the materials from whence this brief compilation is derived, we are mainly indebted to Miner's, Chapman's, and Stone's Histories of Wyoming.

THE VALLEY DESCRIBED.

THE NAME.

THE name of Wyoming was long supposed to mean "a field of blood;" but it has been more correctly found to mean "the large plains." It is derived from *Maughwauwama*, in the dialect of the Delaware Indians, *maughwau* meaning *large*, and *wama* signifying *plains*. Every one will admit that the word has lost nothing under the civilizing process of contraction to which it has been subjected. The name was originally used to designate a much larger extent of country than is embraced within the limits of the valley, and by which it is now appropriated. We shall not, however, introduce any thing in this volume beyond the limits of the valley as it is now known and designated.

THE LOCALITY.

Wyoming is the name given to a beautiful valley, situated along the river Susquehanna, in the north-eastern part of the State of Pennsylvania. It is about three miles wide and twenty-five miles long, and is formed by two ranges of mountains nearly parallel to each other, extending from the northeast to the southwest.

THE MOUNTAINS.

These mountains contain many rocky precipices, and are covered with trees, consisting principally of oak and pine.

The average height of the eastern range is about one thousand feet; that of the western about eight hundred. They are of very irregular form, having elevated points, and deep hollows or openings, which are called "gaps."

THE RIVER.

The Susquehanna enters the valley through a gap in the western mountain, called the "Lackawannock Gap," and, flowing in a serpentine course about twenty miles, leaves the valley through another opening in the same mountain, called the "Nanticoke Gap." These openings are so wide only as to admit of the passage of the river, and are in part faced with perpendicular bluffs of rocks, covered with a thick growth of pine and laurel, which have a very fine appearance when viewed from the river, or from the road which passes along

their bases. The river is in most places about two hundred yards wide, from four to twenty feet deep, and flows with a very gentle current, except at the rapids, or when swelled with rains or melting snows.

THE FALLS.

Near the center of the valley is a rapid called the Wyoming Falls, and another called the " Nanticoke Falls," where the river passes through the Nanticoke Gap. Several tributary streams fall into the river, and, after passing through rocky gaps in the mountains on each side of the valley, form beautiful cascades as they descend into the plain. Those on the northwest side are Toby's Creek, Moses' Creek, and Island Run. On the southeast side are Mill Creek, Laurel Run, Solomon's Creek, and Nanticoke Creek, all of which are sufficient for mills and abound with fish.

THE RIVER PLAINS.

Along the river, and on both sides, are level fertile plains, extending in some places nearly a mile and a half from the margin of the river, where small hills commence stretching to the mountains; the rivers sometimes washing the base of the hills on one side, and sometimes on the other. The surface of the plain in some parts of the valley is elevated about ten feet higher than in other parts, forming a sudden offset or declivity from one to the other. These plains are called the upper and lower " Flats," and spontaneously produce quantities of plums, grapes, many kinds of berries, and a great variety of wild flowers.

COAL.

Throughout the valley and in the sides of the mountains mineral coal, of a very superior quality, is found in great abundance ; it is of the species called anthracite, which burns without smoke, and with very little flame, and constitutes the principal fuel of the inhabitants, as well as their most important article of exportation.

ANCIENT FORTIFICATIONS.

In the valley of Wyoming there exist some remains of ancient fortifications, which appear to have been constructed by a race of people very different in their habits from those who occupied the region when first discovered by the whites. Most of these ruins have been so much obliterated by the operations of agriculture, and inroads which successive floods have made upon them, perhaps for centuries, that their forms cannot now be distinctly traced out. That which remains the most entire was examined during the summer of 1817, and its dimensions carefully ascertained, although from frequent plowing its form had become almost destroyed. It is situated in the township of Kingston, upon a level plain on the north side cf Toby's Creek, about one hundred and fifty feet from its bank, and near its confluence with the Susquehanna. It is of an oval or elliptical form, having its largest diameter from the northwest to the southeast, at right angles to the creek, three hundred and thirty-seven feet, and its shortest diameter from the northeast to the southwest, two hundred and seventy-two feet. On the southwest side appears to have been a gateway about twelve feet wide, opening toward the great eddy of the river into which the creek falls. From present appearances, it consisted probably of only one mound or rampart, which, in height and thickness, appears to have been the same on all sides, and was constructed of earth, the plain on which it stands not abounding in stone. On the outside of the rampart is an intrenchment or ditch, formed probably by removing the earth of which it is composed, and which appears never to have been walled. The creek on which it stands is bounded by a high steep bank on that side, and at ordinary times is sufficiently deep to admit canoes to ascend from the river to the fortification.

When the first settlers came to Wyoming, this plain was covered with its native forest, consisting principally of oak and yellow pine; and the trees which grew in the rampart and in the intrenchment are said to have been as large as those in any other part of the valley; one large oak particularly, upon being cut down, was ascertained to be seven hundred years old. The Indians had no tradition concerning these fortifications, neither did they appear to have any knowledge of the purposes for which they had been constructed. They were, perhaps, erected about the same time with those upon the waters of the Ohio, and probably by a similar people and for similar purposes.

Another fortification similar to this existed on Jacob's Plains, on the upper flats in Wilkes-Barre; but almost every evidence of such structure is now obliterated. The pains-taking and careful explorer of such remains may see, or may think he sees, and cry *Eureka!* but when the spot is reached, imagination must complete the picture.

That the valley was once inhabited by a race superior to that which the pale faces found when they first came there, may safely be concluded. But " what, from whence, and who their sires," and what became of them, it were vain to conjecture: " a heap of dust alone remains," which is occasionally unearthed to show that once " there lived a man."

MR. MINER'S DESCRIPTION.

Mr. Miner, in his exhaustive History of Wyoming, says :—" The valley is diversified by hill and dale, upland and intervale. Its character of extreme richness is derived from the extensive flats, or river-bottoms, which in some places extend from one to two miles back from the river, unrivaled in expansive beauty, unsurpassed in luxuriant fertility. Though now generally cleared and cultivated, to protect the soil from floods, a fringe of trees is left along each bank of the river—the sycamore, the elm, and more especially the black walnut—while here and there, scattered through the fields, a large shell-bark yields a summer shade to the weary laborer, and its autumn fruits to the black and gray squirrel or the rival plow-boy. Pure streams of water come leaping from the mountains, imparting health and pleasure in their course, all of them abounding with the delicious trout. Along these brooks, and in the vales scattered through the uplands, grow the wild plum and the butternut, while, wherever the hand of man has spared it, the native grape may be gathered in unlimited profusion. I have seen a grape-vine bending beneath its purple clusters, one branch climbing a butternut, loaded with fruit ; another branch resting on a wild plum, red with its delicious burden ; the while, growing in their shade, the hazelnut was ripening its rounded kernel.

"Such," he adds, "were common scenes when the white people first came to Wyoming (which seems to have been formed by nature a perfect Indian paradise). Game of every sort was abundant. The quail whistled in the meadow; the pheasant rustled in its leafy covert; the wild duck reared her brood, and bent the reed in every inlet; the red deer fed upon hills, while in the deep forests, within a few hours' walk, was found the stately elk. Several persons now living delight to relate their hunting prowess in bringing down this noblest of our first inhabitants. The rivers yielded at all seasons a supply of fish,—the yellow perch, the pike, the catfish, the bass, the roach, and, in the spring season, myriads of shad."

CHANGES.

The only changes that have been wrought out in the aspects and appearance of the valley are such as the wit and industry of man have projected and accomplished in the so-called improvements of the age. Improvements unquestionably have been made, and great ones too; but why, in carrying them out, it should be necessary to mar (and it would seem to have been done almost wantonly in many instances) the face of nature, by stripping the hill and mountain-side of the growth and groves of trees, where, in former days, was

——————— " many a shade that love might share,
And many a grotto meant for rest,"

but where now is to be seen only a barren, neglected surface—

——————— " doth give us pause."

It is only within a few years that this species of vandalism was undertaken, and pretty nearly accomplished with what yet remained of a former luxuriant growth of beech, maple, walnut, and elm trees, that adorned the western banks of the river below the bridge. But the crime met the recompense of reward ; for the floods came shortly after and utterly obliterated broad acres, washing away an extent which would probably have remained intact, yielding its increase for years to come, as during ages past it had done, had the trees been allowed to remain to protect it from the relentless floods.

THE INDIAN REMAINS.

The whites, upon their discovery and first exploration of the valley, found it occupied by two tribes of

Indians—the Shawanese, on the western bank of the Susquehanna, and the Delawares, on the eastern. The main village of the Delawares was at the bend of the river, just below the town of Wilkes-Barre, and nearly opposite to the first island. The villages of the Shawanese were upon the opposite bank—one not far from the lower end of Ross Hill, and another, the main one, on the Shawanese Flats below.

Upon the site of these, from time to time, either by the washing away of the banks, or in carrying out some *improvement*, numerous discoveries of Indian graves have been made, and the usual relics which they were accustomed to bury with their dead have been brought to light; but these, instead of being carefully kept together and preserved, have been widely scattered, and are now, many of them, hopelessly lost. To show how little value is attached to these remains, I was told of a perfect specimen of Indian pottery, which only the winter before had been broken by some boys who were playing at football with it.

Besides these Indian villages there must have been others, and the " River Bank " at Wilkes-Barre is likely to have been one; for here Indian graves have been frequently discovered, exposed to view either by the washing away of the bank or by leveling it, with a view to *improve* the same; and now that a *horse railroad* is projected, perhaps, in carrying out the plan, more may be discovered. At the bend of the river, about a mile above Mill Creek, are unmistakable evidences that a village formally existed ; for, to this day, numerous pieces of their broken pottery, flint arrow-heads, and other rude relics are to be found there.

THE SHAWANESE.

The Shawanese, whose villages were on the western bank, came into the valley from their former localities, at the " forks of the Delaware " (the junction of the Delaware and Lehigh, at Easton), to which point they had been induced at some remote period to emigrate from their earlier home, near the mouth of the river Wabash, in the " Ohio region," upon the invitation of the Delawares. This was Indian diplomacy, for the Delawares were desirous (not being upon the most friendly terms with the Mingos, or Six Nations) to accumulate a force against those powerful neighbors. But, as might be expected, they did not long live in peace with their new allies : disturbances soon rose between the Shawanese and that portion of the tribe of the Delawares who occupied the country lower down the river. These at length resulted in conflicts so violent, that the Shawanese were compelled to leave the forks of the Delaware, and the whole tribe removed to Wyoming Valley, which they found unoccupied ; here, with no enemy to annoy them, they built their town, upon the west bend of the river, near the lower end of the valley, upon a large plain which still bears the name of the Shawanese Flats, and here they enjoyed many years of repose. The women cultivated corn upon the plains, and the men fished the river and tributary streams, or traversed the surrounding mountains in pursuit of game.

This is the received account, and it is doubtless correct, of the manner in which the Shawanese came into possession of this fair heritage, the valley of Wyoming. But at what exact period they entered upon it is not known.

THE DELAWARES.

It is known, however, when and how the Delawares came afterward to claim with them a joint occupancy of the land, and to make their claim good.

THE SIX NATIONS.

The "Six Nations" were known by the general name of "Mingos." They consisted of the Onandagas, Senecas, Cayugas, Oneydas, Mohawks, and Tuscaroras, and were a powerful, warlike people, who held the surrounding nations in subjection, and claimed a jurisdiction extending from the Connecticut River to the Ohio.   They are described as "a confederacy, who, by their union, courage, and military skill, had reduced a great number of Indian tribes, and subdued a territory more extensive than the whole kingdom of France."

This people claimed the country occupied by the Delawares and Shawanese, and held these tribes subject to their authority.   After the arrival of Penn, he purchased of the Delaware Indians the country along the Delaware River, below the Blue Mountains, supposing those tribes the only legitimate owners; but having been informed of the claim and powers of the Six Nations, he also negotiated a purchase with them.

Difficulties arising between the proprietors and the Delawares respecting the limits of these purchases, the Delawares refused to give possession; and as no accommodation seemed likely to take place, a message was sent from the governor to the Six Nations, informing them of the circumstance, and requesting them to send deputies to meet in council in Philadelphia, with instructions to act upon all subjects in dispute.

Accordingly, in the summer of 1742, the chiefs and principal warriors of the Six Nations, to the number of two hundred and thirty, repaired to Philadelphia, where they met the chiefs of the Delawares, and a general council was opened, in presence of the officers of the colonial government and a large concourse of citizens, in the great hall of the Council House.

THE GENERAL COUNCIL.

The governor, by means of an interpreter, opened the conference upon the part of the proprietaries in a long talk, which set forth that the proprietaries of Pennsylvania had purchased the land in the forks of the Delaware, several years before, of the Delaware tribes, who then possessed them ; that they had afterwards received information that the same lands were claimed by the Six Nations, and a purchase was also made of them ; that in both these purchases the proprietaries had paid the stipulated price ; but that the Delaware Indians had nevertheless refused to give up possession ; and as the Six Nations claimed authority over their country, it had been thought proper to hold a council of all parties, that justice might be done. The chiefs of the Six Nations were then informed, that as they had on all occasions required the government of Pennsylvania to remove any whites that settled on their lands, so now the government of Pennsylvania expected that the Six Nations would cause these Indians to remove from the lands which it had purchased. The deeds from the Indians and drafts of the disputed lands were then produced, and the whole submitted to the consideration of the council.

THE INDIAN PHILIPPIC.

After some deliberation among the different chiefs, Connossatego, a venerable chieftain, arose in the name of all the deputies, and informed the governor "that they saw that the Delawares had been an unruly people, and were altogether in the wrong, and that they had concluded to remove them;" and, addressing himself to the Delawares in a violent manner, he said :—"You deserve to be taken by the hair of the head and shaken till you recover your senses and become sober. We have seen a deed signed by nine of your chiefs, above fifty years ago, for this very land. But how came you to take upon yourselves to sell land at all? We conquered you—we made women of you. You know you are women; and can no more sell lands than women. Nor is it fit that you should have the power of selling lands, since you would abuse it. You have been furnished with clothes, meat, and drink by the goods paid you for it, and now you want it again, like children as you are. But what makes you sell lands in the dark? Did you ever tell us that you had sold these lands? Did we ever receive any part, even the value of a pipe-shank? You have told us a blind story, that you sent a messenger to us to inform us of the sale; but he never came among us, nor have we ever heard any thing about it. But we find that you are none of our blood, but act a dishonest part, not only in this but in other matters. Your ears are ever open to slanderous reports about your brethren. For all these reasons, we charge you to remove instantly: we don't give you liberty to think about it. You are women; take the advice of a wise man and remove instantly. You may return to the other side of the Delaware, where you came from, but we do not know whether, considering how you have demeaned yourselves, you will be permitted to live there, or whether you have not swallowed that land down your throats, as well as the lands on this side. We therefore assign you two places to go to—either to Wyoming or Shamokin. You may go to either of these places, and then we shall have you more under our eyes, and shall see how you behave. Don't deliberate, but remove away, and take this belt of wampum." He then commanded them to leave the council, as he had business to do with the English.

The influence of the Six Nations was too powerful to be disregarded, and the speech of Connossatego had its full effect. The Delawares immediately left the disputed country—some removed to Shamokin and some to Wyoming.

THE ARRIVAL OF THE DELAWARES AT WYOMING.

On their arrival at Wyoming, the Delawares found the valley in possession of the Shawanese; but as these Indians acknowledged the authority of the Six Nations, and knew that the removal of the Delawares was in consequence of their orders, resistance was thought to be inexpedient, and the Delawares, having taken quiet possession of a part of the valley, built their town of Maughwauwama on the east bank of the river, upon the lower flat, below the mouth of a small stream, and nearly opposite the first island above the mouth of Toby's Creek. Such was the origin of the Indian town of Wyoming.

COUNT ZINZENDORF.

Soon after the arrival of the Delawares, and during the same season (the summer of the year 1742), a distinguished foreigner, Count Zinzendorf, of Saxony, visited the valley on a religious mission to the Indians. This nobleman is believed to have been the first white person that ever came to Wyoming. He was the reviver of the ancient church of the United Brethren, and had given protection in his dominions to the persecuted Protestants who had emigrated from

Moravia, thence taking the name of *Moravians*, and who, two years before, had made their first settlement in Pennsylvania.

Upon his arrival in America, Count Zinzendorf manifested great anxiety to have the Gospel preached to the Indians, and although he had heard much of the ferocity of the Shawanese, formed a resolution to visit them. With this view he repaired to Tulpehocken, the residence of Conrad Weiser, a celebrated Indian interpreter, and Indian agent for the Government, whom he wished to engage in the cause, and to accompany him to the Shawanese town. Weiser was too much occupied in business to go immediately to Wyoming; but he furnished the count with letters to a missionary of the name of Mack, and the latter, accompanied by his wife, who could speak the Indian language, proceeded immediately with Zinzendorf on the projected mission.

THE ALARM OF THE SHAWANESE.

The Shawanese appeared to be alarmed at the arrival of the strangers, who pitched their tents on the banks of the river a little below the town, and a council of the chiefs having assembled, the declared purpose of Zinzendorf was deliberately considered. To these unlettered children of the wilderness, it appeared altogether improbable that a stranger should brave the dangers of a boisterous ocean, three thousand miles broad, for the sole purpose of instructing them in the means of obtaining happiness after death, and that too without requiring any compensation for his trouble and expense ; and as they had observed the anxiety of the white people to purchase lands of the Indians, they naturally concluded that the real object of Zinzendorf was either to procure from them the lands at Wyoming for his own uses, to search for hidden treasures, or to examine the country with a view to future conquest. It was accordingly resolved to assassinate him, and to do it privately, lest the knowledge of the transaction should produce a war with the English, who were settling the country below the mountains.

THE RATTLESNAKE LESSON.

Zinzendorf was alone in his tent, seated on a couch of dry weeds, and engaged in writing, when the assassins approached to execute their bloody commission. It was night, and the cool air of September had rendered a small fire necessary to his comfort and convenience. A curtain formed of a blanket, and hung upon pins, was the only guard to the entrance of his tent. The heat of his small fire had aroused a large rattlesnake, which lay in the weeds not far from it; and the reptile, to enjoy it more effectually, crawled slowly into the tent, and passed over one of his legs undiscovered. Without all was still and quiet, except the gentle murmur of the river at the rapids, some distance below. At this moment the Indians softly approached the door of his tent, and, slightly removing the curtain, contemplated the venerable man, too deeply engaged in the subject of his thoughts to notice either their approach, or the snake which lay extended before him. At a sight like this, even the hearts of the savages shrunk from the idea of committing so horrid an act, and, quitting the spot, they hastily returned to the town, and informed their companions that the *Great Spirit* protected the white man, for they had found him with no door but a blanket, and had seen a large rattlesnake crawl over his legs without attempting to injure him.

THE COMING OF THE NANTICOKES.

In May, 1748, large numbers of a tribe of Indians called the Nanticokes, who inhabited the eastern shore of the Chesapeake Bay, having difficulties with the increasing English settlements in that region, removed to Wyoming with their chief sachem, called White. Finding the principal part of the valley in possession of the Shawanese and Delawares, the Nanticokes built their town at the lower end of the valley, on the east bank of the river, just above the mouth of a small creek still called Nanticoke Creek.

EARLY ATTEMPTS AT SETTLEMENTS OF WYOMING BY THE WHITES.

Although Count Zinzendorf was the first white man that ever visited Wyoming, and some of the religious body with which he was connected, and of which he was the head, doubtless followed him to the valley shortly after, it does not appear that the Moravians made any attempt to remain permanently there; they only visited it as missionaries, and in their efforts to Christianize the Indians they met with a measure of success.

The permanent abode of the Brethren had been established at Bethlehem, on the Lehigh, which has been retained by them to the present time.

THE CONNECTICUT COMPANY.

In the summer of 1755, a company procured the consent of the colony of Connecticut for the establishment of a settlement within the limits of a purchase which had been made from the authorities of that colony. This company sent out a number of persons to Wyoming, with their surveyors and agents, to commence a settlement. The conflicting claims of the authorities of Connecticut and Pennsylvania to this region produced strife, and tumults, and even wars, which continued during many years after the possession of the valley had been confirmed to the whites.

CONFLICTING CLAIMS.

The following is a brief account of these conflicting claims : - Connecticut based her claim upon the grant which was derived from the Plymouth Company, of which the Earl of Warwick was president. This grant was made in March, 1631, to Viscount Say and Seal, Lord Brook, and their associates. It was made in the most ample form, and also covered the country west of Connecticut, to the extent of its breadth, thus comprising about one degree of latitude from the Atlantic to the Pacific.* New York, or, to speak more correctly in reference to that period, New Netherlands, being then a Dutch possession, could not be claimed as a portion of these munificent grants ; if for no other reason, for the very good and substantial

---

* "It seems natural to suppose by the terms of these grants, extending to the Western Ocean, that in early times the continent was conceived to be of comparatively little breadth."—PICKERING.

one, that in the grants to the Plymouth Company an exception was made of all such portions of the territory as were " then actually possessed or inhabited by any other Christian prince or state."

The claim of Pennsylvania was based upon the charter granted by King Charles the Second, in 1681, to William Penn, the proprietor and governor of Pennsylvania, his heirs and assigns.

Under each of these grants it was necessary that the Indian title to the lands included in them should be extinguished by purchase *or otherwise*, and this was effectually accomplished—by purchase, treaty, entreaty, *or otherwise*. It is not designed in this compilation to set forth the condition of affairs growing out of conflicting claims to jurisdiction on the part of Pennsylvania and Connecticut ; nor is it at all necessary to argue the question which was in the right. Time has set the matter at rest, for Wyoming may now claim to be the keystone in the arch of the *Keystone* State.

At the date of the first attempts at settlement by the whites (1755), the valley was occupied by portions of three tribes of Indians, viz. :—the Nanticokes, at the foot of the valley upon the eastern side of the river ; the Delawares, above and on the same side ; the Shawanese, upon the western side, as has already been stated, occupying what are now known as the Shawanese Flats, where their principal village existed.

THE GRASSHOPPER WAR.

During the summer of 1755 the Nanticokes, having been induced to unite with other tribes of Indians in a war with the English Colonies, left the valley. A short period after this the Shawanese were driven out of the valley by their more powerful neighbors, the Delawares, and the conflict which resulted in their leaving it grew out of, or was precipitated by, a very trifling incident. While the warriors of the Delawares were engaged upon the mountains in a hunting expedition, a number of squaws or female Indians from Maughwauwame were gathering wild fruits along the margin of the river below the town, where they found a number of Shawanese squaws and their children, who had crossed the river in their canoes upon the same business. A child belonging to the Shawanese having taken a large grasshopper, a quarrel arose among the children for the possession of it, in which their mothers soon took a part; and as the Delaware squaws contended that the Shawanese had no privileges upon that side of the river, the quarrel became general; but the Delawares, being the most numerous, soon drove the Shawanese to their canoes and to their own banks, a few having been killed on both sides. Upon the return of the warriors both tribes prepared for battle, to revenge the wrongs which they considered their wives had sustained.

The Shawanese, upon crossing the river, found the Delawares ready to receive them, and, upon their landing, a dreadful conflict took place between the Shawanese in their canoes and the Delawares on the bank. At length, after great numbers had been killed, the Shawanese effected a landing, and a battle took place about a mile below Maughwauwame, in which many hundred warriors are said to have been killed on both sides; but the Shawanese were so much weakened by landing that they were not able to sustain the conflict, and after the loss of about half their tribe, the remainder were forced to flee to their own side of the river, shortly after which they abandoned their town and removed to the Ohio.

THE DELAWARES TRIUMPHANT.

The Delawares were now masters of Wyoming Valley, and the fame of their triumph, which was supposed to have driven the Shawanese to the west, tended very much to increase their numbers, by calling to their settlement many of those unfriendly Indians near the Delaware who remained on good terms with their Christian neighbors. We have now reached the period when the white man began to assert his supremacy; when he began to increase, and the red man to

decrease ; the result being what has been or is destined
to be the result over the whole extent of the continent.

ATTEMPTS AT SETTLEMENT.

Attempts at settlements were made from time to
time at Wyoming ; the first permanent location of a
colony or town being on the bank of the river, near
Mill Creek, in the year 1762. A small house was
built of logs at the mouth of the creek, which was soon
surrounded by several small cabins, which formed the
residence of the whole colony. They found the valley
covered with woods, except a few acres, the planting-
grounds of the Indians.

The summer was so far advanced when the new
colony arrived that they only prepared a few acres for
wheat, and, as provisions for their sustenance during
the winter could not be procured from the Indians, they
concealed their tools and implements of husbandry,
and in November departed for their former homes in
New England. Early in the spring of 1763 they
returned with their families, and a number of new
emigrants, with a view of commencing a permanent settlement, for which purpose they brought a number of
cattle and hogs, and considerable stores and provisions
for immediate use. They took possession of their

former dwellings at the mouth of the creek, which they found in the same condition as that in which they had been left in the preceding autumn ; and commenced their labors by extending their improvements upon the west side of the river.

INDIAN TREACHERY.

The Indians in the valley were apparently friendly, but this was only the smiling mask which concealed the bitterest passions, for while unsuspicious, and occupied as usual with the labors of the field, the whites were attacked on the 15th of October by a party of Indians, who massacred about twenty persons, took several prisoners, and, having seized upon the live stock, drove it toward their town. Those who escaped hastened to their dwellings, gave the alarm to the families of those who were killed, and the remainder of the colonists, men, women, and children, fled precipitately to the mountains, from whence they beheld the smoke arising from their late habitations, and the savages feasting on the remains of their little property. They had taken no provisions with them except what they hastily seized in their flight ; and now must pass through a wilderness sixty miles in extent before they could reach the Delaware River. They had left brothers, husbands, and sons to the mercy of the savages ; they had no means of defense in case they should be attacked, and they found themselves exposed to the cold winds of autumn without sufficient raiment. With these melancholy recollections and cheerless prospects did the fugitives commence a journey of two hundred and fifty miles on foot. Language can not describe their sufferings as they traveled through the wilderness, destitute of food and clothing, on their way to their former homes.

NEW BANDS OF COLONISTS.

But the sturdy sons of New England were unmoved and unfaltering in their purpose to go up and possess the land.

Colonists and emigrants from this time forward came into the valley, and though they were liable to be startled by the war-whoop of the relentless savages, and to be called from their beds at the dread hour of night to witness the sad sight of peaceful abodes wrapt in flames, or to see father, mother, brother, son, butchered or tortured it might be, and they themselves perhaps compelled to look on the while in speechless agony; they still nerved themselves to bear their misery and privations like men, waiting for those peaceful and happy times which would surely come for them, or, at least, for their children. Noble and brave men, noble and self-sacrificing women! they did not count their lives dear ; they endured bitter hardships ; they have entered upon their rest ; but now their children and their chil-

dren's children are in the quiet and unmolested possession of that for which they so bravely fought and
suffered. The clods of the valley have been heaped
over their resting-places, and, though many of their
graves are unknown and undistinguished, their memory
is cherished, and the story of the privations they
endured, the valor they displayed upon many a well-
fought field, or in limited and personal encounters, is not
forgotten, and their deeds recounted at the winter fire-
side, written out by the historian, and strung in lofty
numbers by great poets. Thus, what with battling
the Indian without, and strifes and contentions within,
growing out of conflicting claims to the territory of
Wyoming, passed years that included in their progress
the war of the Revolution. Although remote from the
scene of its origin, where during its first years the
battle raged, and hoping to enjoy exemption from its
stern realities, the colony struggled along, yet the time
came when Wyoming was destined to receive again the
baptism of blood.

THE STORY OF THE GREAT MASSACRE.

For a season after the breaking out of the war of
the Revolution, Wyoming was allowed a state of com-

parative reposc.　The government of Pennsylvania was changed by the removal of the proprietaries or successors of Penn, and the formation of a new constitution ; and both Connecticut and Pennsylvania had other and more important demands upon their attention than the disputes of rival claimants for a remote and sequestered territory.　Notwithstanding the remoteness of its position, and its peculiar exposure to the attacks of the enemy, rendered more perilous from its contiguity to the territory of the Six Nations, the people of Wyoming were prompt to assume the cause of their country, and, as early as the 1st of August, 1775, in town meeting they voted, "that we will unanimously join our brethren of America in the common cause of defending our country."

THE WYOMING COMPANIES.

A census had been taken, and the whole population of the several towns of the valley now acknowledging the jurisdiction of Connecticut was computed at about two thousand five hundred souls.　Two companies of regular troops, of eighty-two men each, were raised, and commanded by Captains Ransom and Durkee. These companies were mustered and counted as part of the Connecticut levies, and attached to the Connecticut line.　They were moreover efficient soldiers, having been engaged in the brilliant affair of Millstone, the bloody and untoward battles of Brandywine and Germantown, and in the terrible cannonade of Mudbank. It will thus be seen that a considerable draft had been made upon the fighting materials of this colony, and her sons had been called away to fight " freedom's battles " at other and distant points. But, in the mean time, the war was brought home to them—to their doors even.

THE BRITISH AND INDIANS.

The Indians of the Six Nations were brought into the field against the Colonies in the summer of 1777, and shortly after they, in conjunction with the British forces, organized a plan of attack on Wyoming. It was too successful. There were no settlements contiguous to Wyoming upon which they might call for aid in case of sudden emergency. It was distant from any outpost; an isolated community, almost embosomed in the country of a savage enemy. The Six Nations, ever the most dreaded upon the war-path, occupied all the upper branches of the Susquehanna, and were within a few hours' sail of the Plantations.

Thus situated, there had been a conventional understanding between the government and the people of Wyoming, that the regular troops enlisted among them should be stationed there, for the defense of the valley;

but the exigencies of the service required their presence elsewhere, and not only were they ordered away, but other enlistments were made, to the number in all of about three hundred. The only means of defense remaining consisted of militia-men, the greater proportion of whom were either too old or too young for the regular service. No small degree of uneasiness was created, early in 1778, by the conduct of the loyalists yet remaining in the valley. These apprehensions were allayed for a time by messages of peace received from the Indians. But these messages were deceptive, as was ascertained in March by the confessions of one of them, who, while in a state of partial intoxication, revealed their real purposes. They had sent their messenger to Wyoming merely to lull the inhabitants into such a state of security as would enable them to strike a surer blow. And this blow was struck, remorselessly, fatally struck, on the 3d of July, 1778.

THE ATTACK.

The details of this bloody battle; the massacre that ensued; the desolation of the valley that followed; the flight of the survivors down the river, in canoes or hastily constructed rafts, to reach Sunbury, the nearest inhabited post down the Susquehanna; through the great swamp and over the Pocono range of mountains to the settlements on the Delaware, a pathless wilderness, also sixty miles distant; the sufferings that were experienced; the perils that were encountered—are all set forth with painful and harrowing particularity by Mr. Charles Miner, in his HISTORY OF WYOMING. Suffice it here to add that the ruin was complete—" the fiends prevailed;" Wyoming received the baptism of blood; the chalice of woe was held to her lips, and she drank it to the bitter dregs.

THE FLIGHT.

The fugitives generally crossed the mountains to Stroudsburg, where there was a small military post. Their flight was a scene of wide-spread and harrowing terror. The people were scattered, singly, in pairs, and in larger groups, as chance separated them or threw them together in that sad hour of peril and distress. Let the mind picture to itself a single group, flying from the valley to the mountains on the east, and climbing the steep ascent, hurrying onward, filled with terror, despair, and sorrow; the affrighted mother, whose husband had fallen, an infant on her bosom, the child by the hand; an aged parent slowly climbing the rugged steep behind them; hunger presses them severely; in the rustling of every leaf they hear the approaching savage; the deep and dreary wilderness;

the valley all in flames; in the spring-flood of ruin, the star of hope quenched in this blood-shower of savage vengeance. There is no work of fancy in a sketch like this. Indeed, it can not approach the reality. There were in one of the groups that crossed the mountains—one of those that did not perish by the way—one hundred women and children, and but a single man to aid, direct, and protect them. Their sufferings for want, for food, were intense. A number perished on the journey, principally women and children; some died of their wounds; others wandered from their path in search of food, and were lost; and those who survived called the wilderness through which they passed "The Shades of Death," an appellation which it has ever since retained.

Many of the fugitives continued their journey back to Connecticut, ascending the Delaware, and crossing over the Hudson at Poughkeepsie.

THE SAD RETURN.

The fields of Wyoming were waving with heavy burdens of grain ripening for the harvest at the time of the invasion. The enemy, having completed their work of destruction, retired, and, shortly after, considerable numbers of the settlers returned to secure their crops. They also gathered the mutilated and blackened remains of their fallen brothers, and, burying them in two pits, retired. The bodies were found scattered over the battle-field, and where they had fallen in their flight; but the summer's sun had done its work so effectually that they could not be separately identified, and so, in these two pits, ranged as decently as could be, they were buried. The exact locality remained for a long time unknown, and it was not till 1832 that it was discovered, and the bones of those who had fallen in the fight exposed to view; appropriate religious services were solemnized, and other marks of respect extended to their honored remains.

THE MONUMENT.

Measures were instituted to erect a suitable monument on the spot, and the pious determination has been carried out; but it was not till the WOMEN OF WYÔMING took the design in hand that the work was completed. They engaged in it as a labor of love—and having set their hearts to the task, what with donations by them secured, and the results of the labors of willing and industrious hands, ere long "The Wyoming Monument" was erected. An obelisk, about sixty feet in height, bearing the following inscription, has been the result :—

" Near this spot was fought,
On the afternoon of Friday, the third day of July, 1778,
THE BATTLE OF WYOMING,
In which a small band of patriot-Americans,
chiefly the undisciplined, the youthful, and the aged,
spared by inefficiency from the distant ranks of the republic,
led by Col. Zebulon Butler and Col. Nathan Denison,
with a courage that deserved success,
boldly met and bravely fought
a combined British, Tory, and Indian force,
of thrice their number.
Numerical superiority alone gave success to the invader,
and wide-spread havoc, desolation, and ruin
marked his savage and bloody footsteps through the valley.
THIS MONUMENT,
commemorative of these events,
and of the actors in them,
has been erected
over the bones of the slain,
By their descendants, and others who gratefully appreciated
the services and sacrifices of their patriot-ancestors."

It has not been attempted in this compilation of the Romance of the History of Wyoming to include an account of each of the invasions or irruptions that were made upon the early settlers of the valley, or to furnish the details of adventure and suffering and death, in all the horrible and atrocious forms that savage cruelty and vindictiveness could inflict ; but merely to indicate a few of the events which have made the valley a shrine to which history and poetry have dedicated some of their noblest efforts.

The trouble between the conflicting claimants for jurisdiction, after various attempts to fight them out, was arranged by compromises and agreements. The last of the engagements in this war between the Yankees and the Pennymites, in which lives were lost, took place on the 18th of October, 1784. It was long before the settlers were secured in the quiet possession of their lands. But as time passed, wiser counsels prevailed. A compromise was entered upon, in virtue of which the original settlers were secured the possession of their homes, and the long feud was finally healed.

Half a century of peace and prosperity has almost effaced the memory of the troublous years that succeeded, as it will require another half century to efface the memory of the bitter contest from which the country has recently so successfully emerged.

Things have moved along quietly in the valley for years; the development of her mineral wealth has brought in crowding ranks from every people and tongue and kindred; but while she has increased in wealth and material prosperity, the romance of her history closed with the century. The shaft and the big tunnel and the drifts have taken the place of stockade and forts and redoubts; the puffing of the steam-engines and the locomotives, as they go whirling through the valley, give out sounds other than the war-whoop of the savage and the mingled shouts and screams which followed it, and the light from her mountain sides is not that of the cannon or the wide-spread conflagration. Peace is written on her walls and prosperity in all her palaces. One sad episode will close the Romance of the History of Wyoming, viz. :

THE STORY OF FRANCES SLOCUM.

[From Stone's " History of Wyoming." New York, 1841.]

The Slocum family of Wyoming were distinguished for their sufferings during the war of the Revolution, and have been recently brought more conspicuously before the public in connection with the life of a long-lost, but recently discovered sister ; the story of the family opens with tragedy, and ends with romance without fiction.

Mr. Slocum, the father of the subject of the present narrative, was a non-combatant, being a member of the Society of Friends. Feeling himself, therefore, safe from the hostility even of the savages, he did not join the survivors of the massacre in their flight, but remained quietly in his farm—his house remaining in close proximity to the village of Wilkes-Barre.

But the beneficent principles of his faith had little weight with the Indians, notwithstanding the affection with which their race had been treated by the founder of Quakerism in Pennsylvania, the illustrious Penn, and long had the family cause to mourn their imprudence in not retreating from the doomed valley with their neighbors.

It was in the autumn of the same year of the invasion by Butler and Gi-en-gwah-toh, at midday, when the men were laboring in a distant field, that the house of Mr. Slocum was suddenly surrounded by a party of Delawares, prowling about the valley in more earnest search, as it seemed, of plunder, than of scalps or prisoners.

The inmates of the house, at the moment of the surprise, were Mrs. Slocum and four young children, the eldest of whom was a son, aged thirteen; the second a daughter, aged nine; Frances Slocum, aged five; and a little son, aged two years and a half. Near by the house, engaged in grinding a knife, was a young man named Kingsley, assisted in the operation by a lad. The first hostile act of the Indians was to shoot down Kingsley, and take his scalp with the knife he had been sharpening.

The girl nine years old appeared to have had the most presence of mind, for while the mother ran into the edge of the copse of wood near by, Frances attempted to secret herself behind a staircase, and the former seized her little brother, the youngest above mentioned, and ran off in the direction of the fort. True she could not make rapid progress, for she clung to the child, and not even the pursuit of the savages could induce her to drop her charge. The Indians did not pursue her far, and laughed heartily at the panic of the little girl, while they could not but admire her resolution. Allowing her to make her escape, they returned to the house, and, after helping themselves to such articles as they chose, prepared to depart.

The mother seems to have been unobserved by them, although, with yearning bosom, she had so disposed of herself that while she was screened from observation, she could notice all that occurred. But judge of her feelings, at the moment they were about to depart, as she saw little Frances taken from her hiding-place, and preparations made to carry her away into captivity with her brother, already mentioned as being thirteen years old (who, by the way, had been restrained from attempted flight by lameness in one of his feet), and also the lad who a few moments before had been assisting Kingsley at the grindstone. The sight was too much for maternal tenderness to endure. Rushing from her place of concealment, she threw herself upon her knees at the feet of her captors, and, with the most earnest entreaties, pleaded for their restoration. But their bosoms were made of sterner stuff than to yield even to the most eloquent and affectionate of mother's entreaties, and with characteristic stoicism they began to move. As a last resort, the mother appealed to their selfishness, and pointing to the maimed foot of her crippled son, urged as a reason why they should at least relinquish him, the delays and embarrassment he would occasion them on their journey. Being unable to walk, they would, of course, be compelled to carry him the whole distance, or leave him by the way, or take his life. Although insensible to the feelings of humanity, these considerations had the desired effect. The lad was left behind, while, deaf alike to the cries of the mother and the shrieks of the child, Frances was slung over the shoulder of a stalwart Indian with as much indifference as though she were a slaughtered fawn.

The long, lingering look which the mother gave to her child, as her captors disappeared in the forest, was the last glimpse of her sweet features that she ever had. But the vision was for many a long year ever present to her fancy.

As the Indian threw her child over his shoulder, her hair fell over her face, and the mother could never forget how the tears streamed down her cheeks when she brushed it away, as if to catch a last sad look of the mother from whom, her little arms outstretched, she implored assistance in vain.

Nor was this the last visit of the savages to the domicile of Mr. Slocum. About a month thereafter, another horde of the barbarians rushed down from the mountains and murdered the aged grandfather of the little captives, and wounded the lad already lame by the accidental discharge of a ball which lodged in his leg, and which he carried with him to his grave, more than half a century afterward.

These events cast a shadow over the remaining years of Mrs. Slocum. She lived to see many bright and sunny days in that beautiful valley ; bright and sunny, alas ! to her no longer. She mourned the loss of one of whom no tidings, at least during her pilgrimage, could be obtained. After her sons grew up, the youngest of whom, by the way, was born but a few months subsequent to the events already narrated, obedient to the charge of their mother, the most unwearied efforts were made to ascertain what had been the fate of the lost sister. The forests between the Susquehanna and the great lakes, and even the more distant wilds of Canada, were traversed by the brothers in vain, nor could any information respecting her be derived from the Indians. In process of time these efforts were relinquished as hopeless. The lost one might have fallen beneath the tomahawk, or might have proved too tender a flower for transplantation into the wilderness. Conjecture was baffled, and the mother, with a sad heart, sank into the grave, as also did the father, believing, with the Hebrew patriarch, that " the child was not."

The years of a generation passed, and the memory of little Frances was forgotten, save by the two brothers and a sister, who, though advanced in the vale of life, could not forget the family tradition of the lost one. Indeed, it had been the dying charge of their mother that they must never relinquish their exertions to discover Frances. A change now comes over the spirit of the story. It happened that in the course of the year 1835, Colonel Ewing, a gentleman connected with the Indian trade, and also with the public service of the country, in traversing a remote section of Indiana, was overtaken by the night while at a distance from the abodes of civilized man. When it became too dark for him to pursue his way, he sought an Indian habitation, and was so fortunate as to find shelter and a welcome in one of the better sort. The proprietor of the lodge was indeed opulent for an Indian, possessing horses and skins and other comforts in abundance. He was struck, in the course of the evening, by the appearance of the venerable mistress of the lodge, whose complexion was lighter than that of her family ; and as glimpses were occasionally disclosed of her skin, beneath her blanket robe, the Colonel was impressed with the opinion that she was a white woman. Colonel Ewing could converse in the Miami language, to which nation his wife belonged, and after partaking of the best of their cheer, he drew the aged squaw into a conversation, which soon confirmed his suspicions, that she was only an Indian by adoption. Her narrative was substantially as follows :—

" My father's name was Slocum. He resided on the banks of the Susquehanna, but the name of the valley I do not recollect. Sixty winters and summers have gone since I was taken captive by a party of Delawares, while I was playing before my father's house. I was too young to feel, for any length of time, the misery and anxiety which my parents must have experienced. The kindness and affection with which I was treated by my Indian captors, soon effaced my childish uneasiness, and in a short time I became one of them. The first night of my captivity was passed in a cave near the summit of a mountain, but little distance from my father's. That night was the unhappiest of my life, and the impression which it made was the means of indelibly stamping on my memory my father's name and residence. For years we led a roving life. I became accustomed to and fond of their manner of living. They taught me the use of the bow and arrow ; the beasts of the forest supplied me with food. I married a chief of our tribe, whom I had long loved for his bravery and humanity, and kindly did he treat me. I dreaded the sight of a white man ; for I was taught to believe him the implacable enemy of the Indian. I thought he was determined to separate me from my husband and our tribe.

" After I had been a number of years with my husband he died; a part of my people joined the Miamis, and I was among them. I married a Miami, who was called by the pale faces the deaf man. I lived with him a good many winters, until he died. I had by him two sons and two daughters. I am now old and have nothing to fear from the white man. My husband and all my children, but these two daughters, my brothers and sisters have all gone to the Great Spirit, and I shall go in a few moons more. Until this moment I have never revealed my name, or told the mystery that hung over the fate of Frances Slocum."

Such was the substance of the revelation to Colonel Ewing. Still the family at Wyoming were ignorant of the discovery, nor did Colonel Ewing know any thing of them. And it was only by reason of a peculiar providential circumstance that the tidings ever reached their ears. On Colonel Ewing's return to his own home he related the adventure to his mother, who, with the just feelings of a woman, urged him to take some measures to make the discovery known, and at her solicitation he was induced to write a narrative of the case, which he addressed to the postmaster at Lancaster, with a request that it might be published in some Pennsylvania newspaper. But the latter functionary, having no knowledge of the writer, and supposing it might be a hoax, paid no attention to it, and the letter was suffered to remain among the worthless accumulations of the office for two years. It chanced then that the postmaster's wife, in rummaging over the old papers, while ferreting the office one day, glanced her eyes upon this communication. The story excited her interest, and, with the true feelings of a woman, she resolved upon giving the document publicity. With this view she sent it to the neighboring editor, and here again another providential circumstance intervened. It happened that a temperance committee had engaged a portion of the columns of the paper to which the letter of Colonel Ewing was sent, for the publication of an important document connected with that cause, and a large extra number of papers had been ordered for general distribution. The letter was sent forth with the temperance document, and it yet again happened that a copy of this paper was addressed to a clergyman who had a brother residing in Wyoming. Having from that brother heard the story of the captivity of Frances Slocum, he had no sooner read the letter of Colonel Ewing, than he inclosed it to him, and by him it was placed in the hands of Joseph Slocum, Esq., the surviving brother.

Any attempts to describe the sensations produced by this most welcome, most strange, and most unexpected intelligence, would necessarily be a failure. This Mr. Joseph Slocum was the child, two years and a half old, who had been rescued by his intrepid sister, nine years old. That sister also survived, as did the younger brother, living in Ohio. Arrangements were immediately made by the former two to meet the latter in Ohio, and proceed thence to the Miami country and reclaim the long lost and now found sister. "I shall know her if she be my sister," said the elder sister, now going in pursuit, "although she may be painted and jeweled off, and dressed in her Indian blanket, for you, brother, hammered off her finger-nail one day in the blacksmith's shop, when she was four years old." In due season they reached the designated place, and found their sister. But, alas! how changed! instead of the fair-haired and laughing girl, the picture yet living in their imaginations, they found her an aged and thoroughbred squaw in every thing but complexion. But there could be no mistake as to her identity. The elder sister soon discovered the finger-mark. "How came the nail of that finger gone?" "My elder brother pounded it off when I was a little girl, in the shop," she replied. This circumstance was evidence

enough, but other reminiscences were awakened, and
the recognition was complete. How different were the
emotions of the parties! The brothers paced the
lodge in agitation. The civilized sister was in tears.
The other, obedient to the affected stoicism of her
adopted race, was as cold, unmoved, and passionless as
marble.

It was in vain that they besought their sister to
return with them to her native valley, bringing her
children with her if she chose. Every offer and impor-
tunity was declined. She said she was well enough off,
and happy. She had, moreover, promised her husband
on his death-bed never to leave the Indians. Her two
daughters had both been married, but one of them was
a widow. The husband of the other is a half-breed
named Brouillette, who is said to be one of the noblest
looking men of his race. They all have an abundance
of Indian wealth, and her daughters mount their steeds,
and manage them as well as in the days of chivalry did
the rather masculine spouse of Count Robert of Paris.
They lived at a place called the Deaf Man's Village,
nine miles from Peru, in Indiana. But, notwithstanding
the comparative comfort in which they lived, the utter
ignorance of their sister was a subject of painful contemplation to the Slocums. She had entirely forgotten
her native language, and was completely a pagan, having
no knowledge even of the white man's Sabbath.

Mr. Joseph Slocum has since made a second visit to his sister, accompanied by his two daughters. Frances is said to have been delighted with the beauty and accomplishments of her white nieces, but resolutely refused to return to the abode of civilized man. She resided with her daughters in a comfortable log building, but in all her habits and manners, her ideas and thoughts, she is as thoroughly Indian as though not a drop of white blood ran in her veins. She is represented as having manifested, for an Indian, an unwonted degree of pleasure at the return of her brothers; but mother and daughters spurned every persuasive to win them back from the country and manners of their people. Indeed, as all their ideas of happiness are associated with their present mode of life, a change would be productive of little good, so far as temporal affairs are concerned, while, unless they could be won from Paganism to Christianity, their lives would drag along in irksome restraint, if not in pining sorrow.

THE POETRY OF WYOMING.

"Romantic Wyoming! could none be found,
  Of all that rove thy Eden groves among,
To wake a *native* harp's untutored sound,
  And give thy tale of woe the voice of song?
Oh! if description's cold and nerveless tongue
  From stranger harps such hallowed strains could call,
How doubly sweet the descant wild had rung,
  From one who, lingering round 'thy ruined wall,'
  Had plucked thy mourning flowers and wept thy timeless fall."

DRAKE.

CAMPBELL's immortal poem, "Gertrude of Wyoming," beyond any inspiration of the muse which the sad story of her early history furnishes, has spread the name and fame of the Valley of Wyoming to earth's remotest bounds.

This beautiful pastoral was completed in 1808, and published in 1809, and a second edition followed the next year. As soon as it was known that the celebrated author of "The Pleasures of Hope" was employed upon a new poem, and a poem of length, expec-

tation was on tiptoe for its appearance. The information first got wind in the drawing-room of Holland
House. Then the subject was named—then a bit of
the story told by Lord Holland, and a verse or two quoted
by Lady Holland; so that the poem had every adver-
tisement which rank, fashion, reputation, and the poet's
own standing could lend it. The story was liked—then
the meter was named and approved—then a portion
shown; so that the poet had his coterie of fashion and
wits before the public knew even the title of the poem
they were trained up to receive with the acclamation it
deserved. Nor was public expectation disappointed
when it became generally known that the poet had gone
to the banks of the Susquehanna for his poem—had
chosen the desolation of Wyoming for his story, and
the Spenserian stanza for his form of verse. The
poet, however, was still timidly fearful, though he had
the *imprimatur* of Holland House in favor of his poem.

He sent the first printed copy of his poem to Mr.
Jeffrey, of the *Edinburgh Review*. The critic's reply
was favorable. Mrs. Campbell has said that, till he
had received Jeffrey's approbation, her husband was
suffering, to use his own expression, "the horrors of
the damned."

When Jeffrey read "Gertrude," he wrote to the
author, and, with that perspicacity which so well adapted
him for the post of a reviewer, said that the poem

ended abruptly. "Not but that there is great spirit in the description," he added, "but a spirit not quite suitable to the soft and soothing tenor of the poem. The most dangerous faults, however, are your faults of diction. There is still a good deal of obscurity in many passages, and in others a strained and unnatural expression—an appearance of labor and hardness. You have hammered the metal in some places till it has lost all its ductility. These are not great faults, but they are blemishes ; and as dunces will find them out, noodles will see them when they are pointed to. I wish you had courage to correct, or rather avoid them, for with you they are faults of over-finishing, not of negligence. I have another fault to charge you with in private, for which I am more angry than all the rest. Your timidity, or fastidiousness, or some other knavish quality, will not let you give your conceptions glowing, and bold, and powerful, as they present themselves, but you must chasten, and refine, and soften them forsooth, till half their nature and grandeur is chiseled away from them." This was sound advice, friendly, and worthy of the critic. This criticism came home to the poet's faults, which in his better days were too close an adherence to that nicety of verbal polish and disregard of the more manly sense, which are distinguishing traits of university practice in exercise and translation. There were other errors. In "The

Pleasures of Hope," he had introduced panthers on the shores of Lake Erie ; but there is no such animal in the United States—the ounce-like creature, the cougar or jaguar, and the puma, in the South, not being the panthers or leopards of the Old World, but a distinct species. Then the flamingo, the aloe, and palm-tree of the tropics are placed in the severe climate of Pennsylvania, in which plants that flourish well in England perish during the intensity of its winter. These, however, were blemishes which only served to set off the merits of the poem in other respects. The *Edinburgh Review* passed high encomiums upon it ; Dugald Stewart was delighted with it ; Mr. Alison conveyed to the author the admiration of his Edinburgh friends in glowing colors. The poet wrote, in consequence, to a friend :—" Alison's letter is a thing belonging to the heart. Poor Stewart's tears are at present no certain test ; his great, but always susceptible mind is reduced, I dare say, to almost puerile weakness, if I may say it with due reverence to his name (he was suffering under a domestic affliction). Now, let me ask, is it very great ostentation to betray the first symptoms of doubtful success to you ? To you, who are so dear to my heart that you will excuse even its foibles ? I must not exclude your family from hearing something of ' Gertrude.' "

Jeffrey being a Whig, a Whig poet was safe in those

days when in the hands of a Whig critic. Campbell had more to fear from the critical acumen of a Tory writer; but only one number of the *Quarterly Review* had then appeared. If Gifford had dissected " little Miss Gertrude," he might have stopped the sale, for a time, of a new edition; but no critical ferocity could have kept down " Gertrude of Wyoming " for more than one season. But Gifford was prepossessed in favor of Campbell; he liked his versification and his classical correctness; so the poem was intrusted to a friendly hand—one prepossessed, like Gifford, in his favor—the greatest writer and the most generous critic of his age—Sir Walter Scott.

The story is deficient in invention, in which the other works of the poet show that he did not shine. There is enough to carry the simple details required, but no more; and the excellences consist in an all-pervading sweetness and tenderness of handling, in the purity of the sentiment, the richness and splendor, and the pointed vigor displayed in many of the passages. If it does not sparkle like " The Pleasures of Hope," or attract so much by its polish and the artifice of its verse, it possesses a wider range of vision, and touches more deeply the sympathies of the reader.

Campbell was born on the 27th of July, 1777, in Glasgow, and died at Boulogne, on the 15th of June, 1844. His remains were brought to England, and interred in Westminster Abbey, by the side of the ashes of Sheridan, on the 3d of July following.

Halleck visited Wyoming in 1823, and stopped at what was then the principal hotel in Wilkes-Barre, on River Street, below Northampton, and where Louis Philippe and his suite were entertained during their journey through the country in 1795. Halleck's spirited production appeared shortly after his visit to the valley. He was born in Guilford, Connecticut, in 1795, to which quiet town he retired a few years since to spend the evening of his days. It is supposed that the poem of "Wyoming" was partly written in reply to his friend Drake's challenge, entitled "Lines to a Friend," from which we have quoted the beautiful lines at the commencement.

In addition, a few specimens of local poetry are submitted. These "uncouth rhymes," which .

> "Implore the passing tribute of a sigh,"

it can not be doubted, will be acceptable to the antiquarian.

GERTRUDE OF WYOMING.

5

ADVERTISEMENT.

Most of the popular histories of England, as well as of the American war, give an authentic account of the desolation of Wyoming, in Pennsylvania, which took place in 1778, by an incursion of the Indians. The scenery and incidents of the following Poem are connected with that event. The testimonies of historians and travelers concur in describing the infant colony as one of the happiest spots of human existence, for the hospitable and innocent manners of the inhabitants, the beauty of the country, and the luxuriant fertility of the soil and climate. In an evil hour, the junction of European with Indian arms converted this terrestrial paradise into a frightful waste. Mr. Isaac Weld informs us that the ruins of many of the villages, perforated with balls, and bearing marks of conflagration, were still preserved by the recent inhabitants, when he traveled through America, in 1796.

GERTRUDE OF WYOMING.

PART I.

I.

On Susquehanna's side, fair Wyoming!
Although the wild-flower on thy ruined wall
And roofless homes, a sad remembrance bring
Of what thy gentle people did befall:
Yet thou wert once the loveliest land of all
That see the Atlantic wave their morn restore.
Sweet land! may I thy lost delights recall,
And paint thy Gertrude in her bowers of yore,
Whose beauty was the love of Pennsylvania's shore.

II.

Delightful Wyoming! beneath thy skies,
The happy shepherd swains had naught to do
But feed their flocks on green declivities,
Or skim perchance thy lake with light canoe,

From morn till evening's sweeter pastime grew,
With timbrel, when beneath the forests brown
Thy lovely maidens would the dance renew ;
And aye those sunny mountains half-way down
Would echo flagelet from some romantic town.

III.

Then, where of Indian hills the daylight takes
His leave, how might you the flamingo see
Disporting like a meteor on the lakes—
And playful squirrel on his nut-grown tree :
And every sound of life was full of glee,
From merry mock-bird's song, or hum of men ;
While hearkening, fearing naught their revelry,
The wild deer arched his neck from glades, and then,
Unhunted, sought his woods and wilderness again.

IV.

And scarce had Wyoming of war or crime
Heard, but in Transatlantic story rung,
For here the exile met from every clime,
And spoke in friendship every distant tongue :
Men from the blood of warring Europe sprung,
Were but divided by the running brook ;
And happy where no Rhenish trumpet sung,

On plains no sieging mine's volcano shook,
The blue-eyed German changed his sword to pruning-
    hook.

V.

Nor far some Andalusian saraband
Would sound to many a native roundelay—
But who is he that yet a dearer land
Remembers, over hills and far away ?
Green Albin !* what though he no more survey
Thy ships at anchor on the quiet shore,
Thy pellochs † rolling from the mountain bay,
Thy lone sepulchral cairn upon the moor,
And distant isles that hear the loud Corbrechtan roar !‡

VI.

Alas ! poor Caledonia's mountaineer,
That want's stern edict e'er, and feudal grief,
Had forced him from a home he loved so dear !
Yet found he here a home, and glad relief,
And plied the beverage from his own fair sheaf,
That fired his Highland blood with mickle glee :
And England sent her men, of men the chief,

---

* Scotland.   † The Gaelic appellation for the porpoise.
‡ The great whirlpool of the Western Hebrides.

Who taught those sires of Empire yet to be,
To plant the tree of life,—to plant fair Freedom's tree!

VII.

Here were not mingled in the city's pomp
Of life's extremes the grandeur and the gloom ;
Judgment awoke not here her dismal tromp,
Nor sealed in blood a fellow-creature's doom,
Nor mourned the captive in a living tomb.
One venerable man, beloved of all,
Sufficed, where innocence was yet in bloom,
To sway the strife that seldom might befall :
And Albert was their judge in patriarchal hall.

VIII.

How reverend was the look, serenely aged,
He bore, this gentle Pennsylvanian sire,
Where all but kindly fervors were assuaged,
Undimmed by weakness' shade, or turbid ire !
And though, amidst the calm of thought entire,
Some high and haughty features might betray
A soul impetuous once, 'twas earthly fire
That fled composure's intellectual ray,
As Ætna's fires grow dim before the rising day.

IX.

I boast no song in magic wonders rife,
But yet, O Nature! is there naught to prize,
Familiar in thy bosom scenes of life?
And dwells in daylight truth's salubrious skies
No form with which the soul may sympathize?
Young, innocent, on whose sweet forehead mild
The parted ringlet shone in simplest guise,
An inmate in the home of Albert smiled,
Or blessed his noon-day walk—she was his only child.

X.

The rose of England bloomed on Gertrude's cheek;—
What though these shades had seen her birth, her sire
A Briton's independence taught to seek
Far western worlds; and there his household fire
The light of social love did long inspire,
And many a halcyon day he lived to see
Unbroken but by one misfortune dire,
When fate had 'reft his mutual heart—but she
Was gone—and Gertrude climbed a widowed father's
      knee.

XI.

A loved bequest,—and I may half impart,
To them that feel the strong paternal tie,

How like a new existence to his heart
That living flower uprose beneath his eye,
Dear as she was from cherub infancy,
From hours when she would round his garden play,
To time when as the ripening years went by,
Her lovely mind could culture well repay,
And more engaging grew, from pleasing day to day.

XII.

I may not paint those thousand infant charms;
(Unconscious fascination, undesigned!)
The orison repeated in his arms,
For God to bless her sire and all mankind;
The book, the bosom on his knee reclined,
Or how sweet fairy-lore he heard her con,
(The playmate ere the teacher of her mind:)
All uncompanioned else her heart had gone
Till now, in Gertrude's eyes, their ninth blue summer
     shone.

XIII.

And summer was the tide, and sweet the hour,
When sire and daughter saw, with fleet descent,
An Indian from his bark approach their bower,
Of buskined limb, and swarthy lineament;

The red wild feathers on his brow were blent,
And bracelets bound the arm that helped to light
A boy, who seemed, as he beside him went,
Of Christian vesture, and complexion bright,
Led by his dusky guide. like morning brought by
    night.

XIV.

Yet pensive seemed the boy for one so young—
The dimple from his polished cheek had fled ;
When, leaning on his forest bow unstrung,
Th' Oneida warrior to the planter said,
And laid his hand upon the stripling's head :
" Peace be to thee ! my words this belt approve ;
The paths of peace my steps have hither led :
This little nursling, take him to thy love,
And shield the bird unfledged, since gone the parent
    dove.

XV.

" Christian ! I am the foeman of thy foe ;
Our wampum league thy brethren did embrace :
Upon the Michigan, three moons ago,
We launched our pirogues for the bison chase,
And with the Hurons planted for a space,
With true and faithful hands, the olive stalk ;
But snakes are in the bosoms of their race,

And though they held with us a friendly talk,
The hollow peace-tree fell beneath their tomahawk !

XVI.

" It was encamping on the lake's far port,
A cry of Areouski * broke our sleep,
Where stormed an ambushed foe thy nation's fort,
And rapid, rapid whoops came o'er the deep ;
But long thy country's war-sign on the steep
Appeared through ghastly intervals of light,
And deathfully their thunder seem'd to sweep,
Till utter darkness swallowed up the sight,
As if a shower of blood had quenched the fiery fight !

XVII.

" It slept—it rose again—on high their tower
Sprang upward like a torch to light the skies,
Then down again it rained an ember shower,
And louder lamentations heard we rise ;
As when the evil Manitou † that dries
Th' Ohio woods, consumes them in his ire,
In vain the desolated panther flies,

---

* The Indian God of War.   † Manitou, Spirit or Deity.

And howls amidst his wilderness of fire :
Alas! too late, we reached and smote those Hurons
     dire!

XVIII.

" But as the fox beneath the nobler hound,
So died their warriors by our battle brand :
And from the tree we, with her child, unbound
A lonely mother of the Christian land :—
Her lord—the captain of the British band—
Amidst the slaughter of his soldiers lay.
Scarce knew the widow our delivering hand ;
Upon her child she sobbed, and swooned away,
Or shrieked unto the God to whom the Christians
     pray.

XIX.

" Our virgins fed her with their kindly bowls
Of fever-balm and sweet sagamité :
But she was journeying to the land of souls,
And lifted up her dying head to pray
That we should bid an ancient friend convey
Her orphan to his home of England's shore ;—
And take, she said, this token far away,
To one that will remember us of yore,
When he beholds the ring that Waldegrave's Julia
     wore.

XX.

" And I, the eagle of my tribe,* have rushed
With this lorn dove."—A sage's self-command
Had quelled the tears from Albert's heart that gushed ;
But yet his cheek—his agitated hand—
That showered upon the stranger of the land
No common boon, in grief but ill beguiled
A soul that was not wont to be unmanned ;
" And stay," he cried, " dear pilgrim of the wild,
Preserver of my old, my boon companion's child !—

XXI.

" Child of a race whose name my bosom warms
On earth's remotest bounds, how welcome here !
Whose mother oft, a child, has filled these arms,
Young as thyself, and innocently dear ;
Whose grandsire was my early life's compeer.
Ah, happiest home of England's happy clime !
How beautiful e'en now thy scenes appear,
As in the noon and sunshine of my prime !
How gone like yesterday these thrice ten years of time !

---

* The Indians are distinguished, both personally and by tribes, by the
name of particular animals, whose qualities they affect to resemble, either
for cunning, strength, swiftness, or other qualities :—as the eagle, the serpent, the fox, or bear.

XXII.

" And, Julia ! when thou wert like Gertrude now,
Can I forget thee, favorite child of yore?
Or thought I, in thy father's house, when thou
Wert lightest hearted on his festive floor,
And first of all his hospitable door
To meet and kiss me at my journey's end?
But where was I when Waldegrave was no more?
And thou didst, pale, thy gentle head extend
In woes, that e'en the tribe of deserts was thy friend!"

XXIII.

He said—and strained unto his heart the boy :—
Far differently the mute Oneida took
His calumet of peace, and cup of joy ;*
As monumental bronze unchanged his look ;
A soul that pity touched, but never shook ;
Trained from his tree-rocked cradle † to his bier
The fierce extremes of good and ill to brook
Impassive—fearing but the shame of fear—
A stoic of the woods—a man without a tear.

---

* *Calumet of peace.*—The calumet is the Indian name for the ornamental pipe of friendship, which they smoke as a pledge of amity.

† *Tree-rocked cradle.*—The Indian mothers suspend their children in
their cradles from the boughs of trees, and let them be rocked by the
wind.

XXIV.

Yet deem not goodness on the savage stock
Of Outalissi's heart disdained to grow;
As lives the oak unwithered on the rock
By storms above, and barrenness below;
He scorned his own, who felt another's woe;
And ere the wolf-skin on his back he flung,
Or laced his moccasins, in act to go,
A song of parting to the boy he sung,
Who slept on Albert's couch, nor heard his friendly
    tongue.

XXV.

" Sleep, wearied one ! and in the dreaming land
Shouldst thou to-morrow with thy mother meet,
Oh ! tell her spirit, that the white man's hand
Hath plucked the thorns of sorrow from thy feet ;
While I in lonely wilderness shall greet
Thy little footprints—or by traces know
The fountain, where at noon I thought it sweet
To feed thee with the quarry of my bow,
And poured the lotus-horn,* or slew the mountain roe.

---

* From a flower shaped like a horn, which Chateaubriand presumes to
be of the lotus kind, the Indians in their travels through the desert often
find a draught of dew purer than any other water.

XXVI.

" Adieu ! sweet scion of the rising sun !
But should affliction's storms thy blossom mock,
Then come again—my own adopted one !
And I will graft thee on a noble stock :
The crocodile, the condor of the rock,
Shall be the pastime of thy sylvan wars ;
And I will teach thee, in the battle's shock,
To pay with Huron blood thy father's scars,
And gratulate his soul rejoicing in the stars !"

XXVII.

So finished he the rhyme (howe'er uncouth)
That true to nature's fervid feelings ran ;
(And song is but the eloquence of truth :)
Then forth uprose that lone wayfaring man ;
But dauntless he, nor chart, nor journey's plan
In woods required, whose trainèd eye was keen
As eagle of the wilderness, to scan
His path, by mountain, swamp, or deep ravine,
Or ken far friendly huts on good savannas green.

XXVIII.

Old Albert saw him from the valley's side—
His pirogue launched—his pilgrimage begun—

Far, like the red-bird's wing, he seemed to glide ;
Then dived, and vanished in the woodlands dun.
Oft, to that spot by tender memory won,
Would Albert climb the promontory's height,
If but a dim sail glimmered in the sun ;
But never more, to bless his longing sight,
Was Outalissi hailed, with bark and plumage bright.

GERTRUDE OF WYOMING.

PART II.

I.

A VALLEY from the river-shore withdrawn
Was Albert's home, two quiet woods between,
Whose lofty verdure overlooked his lawn ;
And waters to their resting-place serene
Came freshening, and reflecting all the scene
(A mirror in the depth of flowery shelves) ;
So sweet a spot of earth, you might (I ween)
Have guessed some congregation of the elves,
To sport by summer moons, had shaped it for them-
        selves.

II.

Yet wanted not the eye far scope to muse,
Nor vistas opened by the wandering stream ;
Both where at evening Alleghany views,
Through ridges burning in her western beam,
Lake after lake interminably gleam ;

6

And past those settlers' haunts the eye might roam,
Where earth's unliving silence all would seem;
Save where on rocks the beaver built his dome,
Or buffalo remote lowed far from human home.

III.

But silent not that adverse eastern path,
Which saw Aurora's hills th' horizon crown;
There was the river heard, in bed of wrath
(A precipice of foam from mountains brown),
Like tumults heard from some far-distant town;
But softening in approach he left his gloom,
And murmured pleasantly, and laid him down
To kiss those easy curving banks of bloom,
That lent the windward air an exquisite perfume.

IV.

It seemed as if those scenes sweet influence had
On Gertrude's soul, and kindness like their own
Inspired those eyes affectionate and glad,
That seemed to love whate'er they looked upon;
Whether with Hebe's mirth her features shone,
Or if a shade more pleasing them o'ercast
(As if for heavenly musing meant alone),
Yet so becomingly th' expression passed,
That each succeeding look was lovelier than the last.

V.

Nor, guess I, was that Pennsylvanian home,
With all its picturesque and balmy grace,
And fields that were a luxury to roam,
Lost on the soul that look'd from such a face!
Enthusiast of the woods! when years apace
Had bound thy lovely waist with woman's zone,
The sunrise path, at morn, I see thee trace
To hills with high magnolia overgrown,
And joy to breathe the groves, romantic and alone.

VI.

The sunrise drew her thoughts to Europe forth,
That thus apostrophized its viewless scene:
"Land of my father's love, my mother's birth!
The home of kindred I have never seen!
We know not other—oceans are between:
Yet say! far friendly hearts from whence we came,
Of us does oft remembrance intervene?
My mother sure—my sire a thought may claim;
But Gertrude is to you an unregarded name.

VII.

"And yet, loved England! when thy name I trace
In many a pilgrim's tale and poet's song,

How can I choose but wish for one embrace
Of them, the dear unknown, to whom belong
My mother's looks,—perhaps her likeness strong?
Oh, parent! with what reverential awe,
From features of thine own related throng,
An image of thy face my soul could draw!
And see thee once again whom I too shortly saw!"

VIII.

Yet deem not Gertrude sighed for foreign joy;
To soothe a father's couch her only care,
And keep his reverend head from all annoy:
For this, methinks, her homeward steps repair,
Soon as the morning wreath had bound her hair;
While yet the wild deer trod in spangling dew,
While boatman carolled to the fresh-blown air,
And woods a horizontal shadow threw,
And early fox appeared in momentary view.

IX.

Apart there was a deep untrodden grot,
Where oft the reading hours sweet Gertrude wore;
Tradition had not named its lonely spot;
But here (methinks) might India's sons explore

Their fathers' dust,* or lift perchance of yore,
Their voice to the great Spirit :—rocks sublime
To human art a sportive semblance bore,
And yellow lichens colored all the clime,
Like moonlight battlements, and towers decayed by
      time.

x.

But high in amphitheatre above,
Gay tinted woods their massy foliage threw :
Breathed but an air of heaven, and all the grove
As if instinct with living spirit grew,
Rolling its verdant gulfs of every hue ;
And now suspended was the pleasing din,
Now from a murmur faint it swelled anew,
Like the first note of organ heard within
Cathedral aisles,—ere yet its symphony begin.

xi.

It was in this lone valley she would charm
The lingering noon, where flowers a couch had strewn ;
Her cheek reclining, and her snowy arm

---

   * It is a custom of the Indian tribes to visit the tombs of their ancestors, in the cultivated parts of America, who have been buried for upwards of a century.

On hillock by the palm-tree half o'ergrown :
And aye that volume on her lap is thrown,
Which every heart of human mould endears ;
With Shakspeare's self she speaks and smiles alone,
And no intruding visitation fears,
To shame the unconscious laugh, or stop her sweetest
  tears.

XII.

And naught within the grove was seen or heard
But stock-doves plaining through its gloom profound,
Or winglet of the fairy humming-bird,
Like atoms of the rainbow fluttering round ;
When lo ! there entered to its inmost ground
A youth, the stranger of a distant land ;
He was, to weet, for eastern mountains bound ;
But late th' equator suns his cheek had tanned,
And California's gales his roving bosom fanned.

XIII.

A steed, whose rein hung loosely o'er his arm,
He led dismounted ; ere his leisure pace,
Amid the brown leaves, could her ear alarm,
Close he had come, and worshipped for a space
Those downcast features :—she her lovely face

Uplift on one, whose lineaments and frame
Wore youth and manhood's intermingled grace;
Iberian seemed his boot—his robe the same,
And well the Spanish plume his lofty looks became.

XIV.

For Albert's home he sought—her finger fair
Has pointed where the father's mansion stood.
Returning from the copse, he soon was there:
And soon has Gertrude hied from dark, green wood;
Nor joyless, by the converse, understood
Between the man of age and pilgrim young,
That gay congeniality of mood,
And early liking from acquaintance sprung:
Full fluently conversed their guest in England's tongue.

XV.

And well could he his pilgrimage of taste
Unfold,—and much they loved his fervid strain,
While he each fair variety retraced
Of climes, and manners, o'er the eastern main.
Now happy Switzer's hills,—romantic Spain,—
Gay lilied fields of France,—or, more refined,
The soft Ausonia's monumental reign;
Nor less each rural image he designed
Than all the city's pomp and home of human kind.

XVI.

Anon some wilder portraiture he draws ;
Of nature's savage glories he would speak,—
The loneliness of earth that overawes,—
Where, resting by some tomb of old cacique,
The lama-driver on Peruvia's peak
Nor living voice nor motion marks around ;
But storks that to the boundless forest shriek,
Or wild-cane arch high flung o'er gulf profound,*
That fluctuates when the storms of El Dorado sound.

XVII.

Pleased with his guest, the good man still would ply
Each earnest question, and his converse court ;
But Gertrude, as she eyed him, knew not why
A strange and troubling wonder stopped her short.
" In England thou hast been,—and, by report,
An orphan's name (quoth Albert) mayst have known.
Sad tale !—when latest fell our frontier fort,
One innocent—one soldier's child—alone
Was spared, and brought to me, who loved him as my
     own.—

---

* The bridges over narrow streams in many parts of Spanish America
are said to be built of cane, which, however strong to support the pas-
senger, are yet waved in the agitation of the storm, and frequently add to
the effect of a mountainous and picturesque scenery.

XVIII.

" Young Henry Waldegrave! three delightful years
These very walls his infant sports did see :
But most I loved him when his parting tears
Alternately bedewed my child and me ;
His sorest parting, Gertrude, was from thee ;
Nor half its grief his little heart could hold :
By kindred he was sent for o'er the sea ;
They tore him from us when but twelve years old,
And scarcely for his loss have I been yet consoled !"

XIX.

His face the wanderer hid—but could not hide
A tear, a smile, upon his cheek that dwell ;—
" And speak ! mysterious stranger !" (Gertrude cried)
" It is !—it is !—I knew—I knew him well !
'Tis Waldegrave's self, of Waldegrave come to tell !"
A burst of joy the father's lips declare,
But Gertrude speechless on his bosom fell ;
At once his open arms embraced the pair,—
Was never group more blest in this wide world of care.

XX.

" And will ye pardon then (replied the youth)
Your Waldegrave's feigned name, and false attire ?

I durst not in the neighborhood, in truth,
The very fortunes of your house inquire,
Lest one that knew me might some tidings dire
Impart, and I my weakness all betray ;
For had I lost my Gertrude and my sire,
I meant but o'er your tombs to weep a day :
Unknown I meant to weep, unknown to pass away.

XXI.

" But here ye live,—ye bloom,—in each dear face,
The changing hand of time I may not blame ;
For there, it hath but shed more reverend grace,
And here, of beauty perfected the frame :
And well I know your hearts are still the same—
They could not change—ye look the very way
As when an orphan first to you I came.
And have ye heard of my poor guide, I pray ?
Nay, wherefore weep ye, friends, on such a joyous
　　　day ?"

XXII.

" And art thou here ? or is it but a dream ?
And wilt thou, Waldegrave, wilt thou leave us more ?"—
" No, never ! thou that yet dost lovelier seem
Than aught on earth—than e'en thyself of yore—
I will not part thee from thy father's shore ;

But we will cherish him with mutual arms,
And hand in hand again the path explore,
Which every ray of young remembrance warms,
While thou shalt be my own, with all thy truth and
   charms !"

XXIII.

At morn, as if beneath a galaxy
Of over-arching groves in blossoms white,
Where all was odorous scent and harmony,
And gladness to the heart, nerve, ear, and sight :
There, if, oh gentle Love ! I read aright
The utterance that sealed thy sacred bond,
'Twas listening to these accents of delight,
She hid upon his breast those eyes, beyond
Expression's power to paint, all languishingly fond.

XXIV.

" Flower of my life, so lovely, and so lone !
Whom I would rather in this desert meet,
Scorning and scorn'd by fortune's power, than own
Her pomp and splendors lavished at my feet !
Turn not from me thy breath, more exquisite
Than odors cast on heaven's own shrine—to please—
Give me thy love, than luxury more sweet,
And more than all the wealth that loads the breeze,
When Coromandel's ships return from Indian seas."

XXV.

Then would that home admit them—happier far
Than grandeur's most magnificent saloon,
While, here and there, a solitary star
Flushed in the darkening firmament of June ;
And silence brought the soul-felt hour, full soon,
Ineffable, which I may not portray ;
For never did the hymenean moon
A paradise of hearts more sacred sway,
In all that slept beneath her soft voluptuous ray.

GERTRUDE OF WYOMING.

—

PART III.

I.

O Love! in such a wilderness as this,
Where transport and security entwine,
Here is the empire of thy perfect bliss,
And here thou art a god indeed divine.
Here shall no forms abridge, no hours confine
The views, the walks, that boundless joy inspire!
Roll on, ye days of raptured influence, shine!
Nor, blind with ecstasy's celestial fire,
Shall love behold the spark of earth-born time expire.

II.

Three little moons, how short! amidst the grove
And pastoral savannas they consume!
While she, beside her buskined youth to rove,
Delights in fancifully wild costume,
Her lovely brow to shade with Indian plume;

And forth in hunter-seeming vest they fare ;
But not to chase the deer in forest gloom ;
'Tis but the breath of heaven—the blessed air—
And interchange of hearts unknown, unseen to share.

III.

What though the sportive dog oft round them note,
Or fawn, or wild bird bursting on the wing ;
Yet who, in love's own presence, would devote
To death those gentle throats that wake the spring,
Or writhing from the brook its victim bring ?
No !—nor let fear one little warbler rouse ;
But, fed by Gertrude's hand, still let them sing,
Acquaintance of her path, amidst the boughs,
That shade e'en now her love, and witnessed first her
      vows.

IV.

Now labyrinths, which but themselves can pierce,
Methinks, conduct them to some pleasant ground,
Where welcome hills shut out the universe,
And pines their lawny walk encompass round ;
There, if a pause delicious converse found,
'Twas but when o'er each heart the idea stole
(Perchance awhile in joy's oblivion drowned),
That come what may, while life's glad pulses roll,
Indissolubly thus should soul be knit to soul.

V.

And in the visions of romantic youth,
What years of endless bliss are yet to flow!
But, mortal pleasure, what art thou in truth?
The torrent's smoothness, ere it dash below!
And must I change my song? and must I show,
Sweet Wyoming! the day when thou wert doomed,
Guiltless, to mourn thy loveliest bowers laid low?
When where of yesterday a garden bloomed,
Death overspread his pall, and blackening ashes
     gloomed!

VI.

Sad was the year, by proud oppression driven,
When Transatlantic Liberty arose,
Not in the sunshine and the smile of heaven,
But wrapt in whirlwinds, and begirt with woes,
Amidst the strife of fratricidal foes;
Her birth-star was the light of burning plains;*
Her baptism is the weight of blood that flows
From kindred hearts—the blood of British veins—
And famine tracks her steps, and pestilential pains.

---

* Alluding to the miseries that attended the American civil war.

VII.

Yet, ere the storm of death had raged remote,
Or siege unseen in heaven reflects its beams,
Who now each dreadful circumstance shall note,
That fills pale Gertrude's thoughts, and nightly dreams?
Dismal to her the forge of battle gleams
Portentous light! and music's voice is dumb;
Save where the fife its shrill reveillé screams,
Or midnight streets re-echo to the drum,
That speaks of maddening strife, and blood-stained fields
     to come.

VIII.

It was in truth a momentary pang;
Yet how comprising myriad shapes of woe!
First when in Gertrude's ear the summons rang,
A husband to the battle doomed to go!
" Nay, meet not thou (she cries) thy kindred foe,
But peaceful let us seek fair England's strand!"
" Ah, Gertrude! thy belovèd heart, I know,
Would feel like mine the stigmatizing brand,
Could I forsake the cause of Freedom's holy band!

IX.

" But shame—but flight—a recreant's name to prove,
To hide in exile ignominious fears;

Say, e'en if this I brooked—the public love
Thy father's bosom to his home endears :
And how could I his few remaining years,
My Gertrude, sever from so dear a child ?"
So, day by day, her boding heart he cheers :
At last that heart to hope is half beguiled,
And, pale through tears suppressed, the mournful beauty
    smiled.

X.

Night came—and in their lighted bower, full late,
The joy of converse had endured—when, hark !
Abrupt and loud a summons shook their gate ;
And, heedless of the dog's obstreperous bark,
A form had rushed amidst them from the dark,
And spread his arms—and fell upon the floor :
Of aged strength his limbs retained the mark ;
But desolate he looked, and famished, poor,
As ever shipwrecked wretch lone left on desert shore.

XI.

Uprisen, each wondering brow is knit and arched :
A spirit from the dead they deem him first :
To speak he tries ; but quivering, pale, and parched,
From lips, as by some powerless dream accursed,
Emotions unintelligible burst ;

7

And long his filmèd eye is red and dim ;
At length the pity-proffered cup his thirst
Had half assuaged, and nerved his shuddering limb,
When Albert's hand he grasped ;—but Albert knew not
     him.

XII.

" And hast thou then forgot" (he cried, forlorn,
And eyed the group with half-indignant air),
" Oh ! hast thou, Christian chief, forgot the morn
When I with thee the cup of peace did share ?
Then stately was this head, and dark this hair,
That now is white as Appalachia's snow ;
But, if the weight of fifteen years' despair
And age hath bowed me, and the torturing foe,
Bring me my boy—and he will his deliverer know !"

XIII.

It was not long, with eyes and heart of flame,
Ere Henry to his loved Oneida flew :
" Bless thee, my guide !"—but backward, as he came,
The chief his old bewildered head withdrew,
And grasped his arm, and looked and looked him
     through.
'Twas strange—nor could the group a smile control—
The long, the doubtful scrutiny to view :—

At last delight o'er all his features stole,
"It is—my own," he cried, and clasped him to his
    soul.

XIV.

"Yes! thou recall'st my pride of years, for then
The bowstring of my spirit was not slack,
When, spite of woods, and floods, and ambushed men,
I bore thee like the quiver on my back,
Fleet as the whirlwind hurries on the rack;
Nor foeman then, nor cougar's crouch I feared,*
For I was strong as mountain cataract:
And dost thou not remember how we cheered
Upon the last hill-top, when white men's huts ap-
    peared?

XV.

"Then welcome be my death-song, and my death,
Since I have seen thee, and again embraced."
And longer had he spent his toil-worn breath,
But, with affectionate and eager haste,
Was every arm outstretched around their guest,
To welcome and to bless his aged head.
Soon was the hospitable banquet placed;

---

* Cougar, the American tiger.

And Gertrude's lovely hands a balsam shed
On wounds with fevered joy that more profusely bled.

XVI.

" But this is not a time,"—he started up,
And smote his breast with woe-denouncing hand—
" This is no time to fill the joyous cup ;
The   Mammoth   comes,—the   foe,—the   Monster
      Brant,*—
With all his howling desolating band ;—
These eyes have seen their blade and burning pine
Awake at once, and silence half your land.
Red is the cup they drink ; but not with wine :
Awake, and watch to-night, or see no morning shine !

XVII.

" Scorning to wield the hatchet for his bribe,
'Gainst Brant himself I went to battle forth :
Accursed Brant ! he left of all my tribe
Nor man, nor child, nor thing of living birth :
No ! not the dog, that watched my household hearth,
Escaped that night of blood, upon our plains !
All perished !—I alone am left on earth !

---

* Brant was the leader of those Mohawks, and other savages, who laid
waste this part of Pennsylvania. Vide the note at the end of this poem.

To whom nor relative nor blood remains ;
No !—not a kindred drop that runs in human veins !

XVIII.

" But go !—and rouse your warriors ;—for, if right
These old bewildered eyes could guess, by signs
Of striped and starred banners, on yon height
Of eastern cedars, o'er the creek of pines—
Some fort embattled by your country shines :
Deep roars the innavigable gulf below
Its squarèd rocks, and palisaded lines.
Go ! seek the light its warlike beacons show ;
Whilst I in ambush wait, for vengeance and the foe !"

XIX.

Scarce had he uttered—when heaven's verge extreme
Reverberates the bomb's descending star,—
And sounds that mingled laugh,—and shout,—and
    scream,—
To freeze the blood, in one discordant jar,
Rung to the pealing thunderbolts of war.
Whoop after whoop with rack the ear assailed !
As if unearthly fiends had burst their bar ;
While rapidly the marksman's shot prevailed :—
And aye, as if for death, some lonely trumpet wailed.

XX.

Then looked they to the hills, where fire o'erhung
The bandit groups, in one Vesuvian glare ;
Or swept, far seen, the tower, whose clock unrung,
Told legible that midnight of despair.
She faints,—she falters not,—the heroic fair,—
As he the sword and plume in haste arrayed.
One short embrace—he clasped his dearest care—
But hark ! what nearer war-drum shakes the glade?
Joy, joy ! Columbia's friends are tramping through the
     shade !

XXI.

Then came of every race the mingled swarm,
Far rung the groves, and gleamed the midnight grass,
With flambeau, javelin, and naked arm ;
As warriors wheeled their culverins of brass,
Sprung from the woods, a bold athletic mass,
Whom virtue fires, and liberty combines :
And first the wild Moravian yagers pass ;
His plumèd host the dark Iberian joins—
And Scotia's sword beneath the Highland thistle shines.

XXII.

And in, the buskined hunters of the deer,
To Albert's home, with shout and cymbal throng :

Roused by their warlike pomp, and mirth, and cheer,
Old Outalissi woke his battle-song,
And, beating with his war-club cadence strong,
Tells how his deep-stung indignation smarts,
Of them that wrapt his house in flames, ere long
To whet a dagger on their stony hearts,
And smile avenged ere yet his eagle spirit parts.

XXIII.

Calm, opposite the Christian father rose,
Pale on his venerable brow its rays
Of martyr light the conflagration throws ;
One hand upon his lovely child he lays,
And one the uncovered crowd to silence sways ;
While, though the battle flash is faster driven,—
Unawed, with eye unstartled by the blaze,
He for his bleeding country prays to Heaven—
Prays that the men of blood themselves may be forgiven.

XXIV.

Short time is now for gratulating speech :
And yet, beloved Gertrude, ere began
Thy country's flight, yon distant towers to reach,
Looked not on thee the rudest partisan
With brow relaxed to love ? And murmurs ran,
As round and round their willing ranks they drew,

From beauty's sight to shield the hostile van.
Grateful, on them a placid look she threw,
Nor wept, but as she bade her mother's grave adieu!

XXV.

Past was the flight, and welcome seemed the tower, ,
That like a giant standard-bearer frowned
Defiance on the roving Indian power.
Beneath, each bold and promontory mound
With embrasure embossed, and armor crowned,
An arrowy frieze, and wedged ravelin,
Wove like a diadem its tracery round
The lofty summit of that mountain green ;
Here stood secure the group, and eyed a distant scene,—

XXVI.

A scene of death ! where fires beneath the sun,
And blended arms, and white pavilions glow ;
And for the business of destruction done,
Its requiem the war-horn seemed to blow :
There, sad spectatress of her country's woe !
The lovely Gertrude, safe from present harm,
Had laid her cheek, and clasped her hands of snow
On Waldegrave's shoulder, half within his arm
Enclosed, that felt her heart, and hushed its wild alarm !

XXVII.

But short that contemplation—sad and short
The pause to bid each much-loved scene adieu!
Beneath the very shadow of the fort,
Where friendly swords were drawn, and banners flew,
Ah! who could deem that foot of Indian crew
Was near?—yet there, with lust of murderous deeds,
Gleamed like a basilisk, from woods in view,
The ambushed foeman's eye—his volley speeds,
And Albert—Albert falls! the dear old father bleeds!

XXVIII.

And tranced in giddy horror, Gertrude swooned;
Yet, while she clasps him lifeless to her zone,
Say, burst they, borrowed from her father's wound,
These drops?—Oh God! the life-blood is her own!
And faltering, on her Waldegrave's bosom thrown,
" Weep not, O love!"—she cries, " to see me bleed—
Thee, Gertrude's sad survivor, thee alone
Heaven's peace commiserate; for scarce I heed
These wounds;—yet thee to leave is death, is death
     indeed!

XXIX.

" Clasp me a little longer, on the brink
Of fate! while I can feel thy dear caress;

And when this heart hath ceased to beat—oh think,
And let it mitigate thy woe's excess,
That thou hast been to me all tenderness,
And friend to more than human friendship just.
Oh! by that retrospect of happiness,
And by the hopes of an immortal trust,
God shall assuage thy pangs when I am laid in dust!

XXX.

"Go, Henry, go not back, when I depart;
The scene thy bursting tears too deep will move,
Where my dear father took thee to his heart,
And Gertrude thought it ecstasy to rove
With thee, as with an angel, through the grove
Of peace, imagining her lot was cast
In heaven; for ours was not like earthly love.
And must this parting be our very last?
No! I shall love thee still, when death itself is past.

XXXI.

" Half could I bear, methinks, to leave this earth,
And thee, more loved than aught beneath the sun,
If I had lived to smile but on the birth
Of one dear pledge;—but shall there then be none,
In future times—no gentle little one,

To clasp thy neck, and look, resembling me?
Yet seems it, e'en while life's last pulses run,
A sweetness in the cup of death to be,
Lord of my bosom's love! to die beholding thee!"

XXXII.

Hushed were his Gertrude's lips! but still their bland
And beautiful expression seemed to melt
With love that could not die! and still his hand
She presses to the heart no more that felt.
Ah, heart! where once each fond affection dwelt,
And features yet that spoke a soul more fair.
Mute, gazing, agonizing as he knelt,—
Of them that stood encircling his despair,
He heard some friendly words ;— but knew not what
    they were.

XXXIII.

For now, to mourn their judge and child, arrives
A faithful band.   With solemn rites between,
'Twas sung, how they were lovely in their lives,
And in their deaths had not divided been.
Touched by the music, and the melting scene,
Was scarce one tearless eye amidst the crowd :—
Stern warriors, resting on their swords, were seen
To veil their eyes, as passed each much-loved shroud—
While woman's softer soul in woe dissolved aloud.

XXXIV.

Then mournfully the parting bugle bid
Its farewell o'er the grave of worth and truth ;
Prone to the dust, afflicted Waldegrave hid
His face on earth ;—him watched, in gloomy ruth,
His woodland guide : but words had none to soothe
The grief that knew not consolation's name :
Casting his Indian mantle o'er the youth,
He watched, beneath its folds, each burst that came
Convulsive, ague-like, across his shuddering frame !

XXXV.

"And I could weep ;"—th' Oneida chief
His descant wildly thus begun :
" But that I may not stain with grief
The death-song of my father's son,
Or bow this head in woe !
For by my wrongs, and hy my wrath !
To-morrow Areouski's breath
(That fires yon heaven with storms of death)
Shall light us to the foe ;
And we shall share, my Christian boy !
The foeman's blood, the avenger's joy !

XXXVI.

" But thee, my flower, whose breath was given
By milder genii o'er the deep,

The spirits of the white man's heaven
Forbid not thee to weep:—
Nor will the Christian host,
Nor will thy father's spirit grieve,
To see thee, on the battle's eve,
Lamenting, take a mournful leave
Of her who loved thee most:
She was the rainbow to thy sight!
Thy sun—thy heaven—of lost delight!

XXXVII.

" To-morrow let us do or die!
But when the bolt of death is hurled,
Ah! whither then with thee to fly,
Shall Outalissi roam the world?
Seek we thy once-loved home?
The hand is gone that cropped its flowers:
Unheard their clock repeats its hours!
Cold is the hearth within their bowers!.
And should we thither roam,
Its echoes, and its empty tread,
Would sound like voices from the dead!

XXXVIII.

"Or shall we cross yon mountains blue,
Whose streams my kindred nation quaffed,

And by my side, in battle true,
A thousand warriors drew the shaft ?
Ah ! there in desolation cold,
The desert serpent dwells alone,
Where grass o'ergrows each mouldering bone,
And stones themselves to ruin grown,
Like me, are death-like old.
Then seek we not their camp,—for there
The silence dwells of my despair !

XXXIX.

" But hark, the trump !—to-morrow thou
In glory's fires shalt dry thy tears :
E'en from the land of shadows now
My father's awful ghost appears,
Amidst the clouds that round us roll !
He bids my soul for battle thirst—
He bids me dry the last --the first—
The only tears that ever burst
From Outalissi's soul ;
Because I may not stain with grief
The death-song of an Indian chief !"

WYOMING.*

BY FITZ-GREENE HALLECK.

" Dites si la Nature n'a pas fait ce beau pays pour une Julie, pour une Claire, et pour un St. Preux, mais ne les y cherchez pas."

ROUSSEAU.

I.

THOU com'st, in beauty, on my gaze at last,
" On Susquehanna's side, fair Wyoming !"
Image of many a dream, in hours long past,
When life was in its bud and blossoming,
And waters, gushing from the fountain spring
Of pure enthusiast thought, dimmed my young eyes,
As by the poet borne, on unseen wing,
I breathed, in fancy, 'neath thy cloudless skies,
The summer's air, and heard her echoed harmonies.

II.

I then but dreamed : thou art before me now,
In life, a vision of the brain no more.

---

* The allusion in the following stanzas can be understood by those only who have read Campbell's beautiful poem, " GERTRUDE OF WYOMING :" but who has not read it ?

I've stood upon the wooded mountain's brow,
That beetles high thy lovely valley o'er ;
And now, where winds thy river's greenest shore,
Within a bower of sycamores am laid ;
And winds, as soft and sweet as ever bore
The fragrance of wild flowers through sun and shade,
Are singing in the trees, whose low boughs press my
  head.

III.

Nature hath made thee lovelier than the power
Even of Campbell's pen hath pictured : he
Had woven, had he gazed one sunny hour
Upon thy smiling vale, its scenery
With more of truth, and made each rock and tree
Known like old friends, and greeted from afar :
And there are tales of sad reality,
In the dark legends of thy border war,
With woes of deeper tint than his own Gertrude's are.

IV.

But where are they, the beings of the mind,
The bard's creations, moulded not of clay,
Hearts to strange bliss and suffering assigned—
Young Gertrude, Albert, Waldegrave—where are
  they ?

We need not ask.   The people of to-day
Appear good, honest, quiet men enough,
And hospitable too—for ready pay ;
With manners like their roads, a little rough,
And hands whose grasp is warm and welcoming, though
    tough.

v.

Judge   *   *   *,   who keeps the toll-bridge gate,
And the town records, is the Albert now
Of Wyoming : like him, in church and state,
Her Doric column ; and upon his brow
The thin hairs, white with seventy winters' snow,
Look patriarchal.   Waldegrave 'twere in vain
To point out here, unless in yon scare-crow,
That stands full-uniformed upon the plain,
To frighten flocks of crows and blackbirds from the
    grain.

VI.

For he would look particularly droll
In his " Iberian boot " and " Spanish plume,"
And be the wonder of each Christian soul,
As of the birds that scare-crow and his broom.
But Gertrude, in her loveliness and bloom,
Hath many a model here ; for woman's eye,

8

In court or cottage, wheresoe'er her home,
Hath a heart-spell too holy and too high
To be o'erpraised even by her worshipper—Poesy.

VII.

There's one in the next field—of sweet sixteen—
Singing and summoning thoughts of beauty born
In heaven—with her jacket of light green,
" Love-darting eyes, and tresses like the morn,"
Without a shoe or stocking—hoeing corn.
Whether, like Gertrude, she oft wanders there,
With Shakspeare's volume in her bosom borne,
I think is doubtful.   Of the poet-player
The maiden knows no more than Cobbett or Voltaire.

VIII.

There is a woman, widowed, gray, and old,
Who tells you where the foot of Battle stepped
Upon their day of massacre.   She told
Its tale, and pointed to the spot, and wept,
Whereon her father and five brothers slept
Shroudless, the bright-dreamed slumbers of the brave,
When all the land a funeral mourning kept.
And there, wild laurels planted on the grave
By Nature's hand, in air their pale red blossoms wave.

IX.

And on the margin of yon orchard hill
Are marks where time-worn battlements have been,
And in the tall grass traces linger still
Of " arrowy frieze and wedgèd ravelin."
Five hundred of her brave that valley green
Trod on the morn in soldier-spirit gay ;
But twenty lived to tell the noonday scene—
And where are now the twenty ? Passed away.
Has Death no triumph-hours, save on the battle-day ?

LOCAL POETRY.

WYOMING MASSACRE.

1. KIND Heaven, assist the trembling muse,
    While she attempts to tell
Of poor Wyoming's overthrow,
    By savage sons of hell.

2. One hundred whites, in painted hue
    Whom Butler there did lead,
Supported by a barb'rous crew
    Of the fierce savage breed.

3. The last of June the siege began,
    And several days it held,
While many a brave and valiant man
    Lay slaughtered on the field.

4. Our troops marched out from Forty Fort,
    The third day of July,
Three hundred strong, they march along,
    The fate of war to try.

5. But oh! alas! three hundred men
    Is much too small a band,
  To meet eight hundred men complete,
    And make a glorious stand.

6. Four miles they marchèd from the Fort
    Their enemy to meet,
  Too far indeed did Butler lead,
    To keep a safe retreat.

7. And now the fatal hour is come—
    They bravely charge the foe,
  And they with ire, returned the fire,
    Which proved our overthrow.

8. Some minutes they sustained the fire,
    But ere they were aware
  They were encompassed all around,
    Which proved a fatal snare.

9. And then they did attempt to fly,
    But all was now in vain;
  Their little host—by far the most—
    Was by those Indians slain.

10. And as they fly, for quarters cry;
    Oh hear! indulgent Heaven!

Hard to relate—their dreadful fate,
  No quarters must be given.

11. With bitter cries and mournful sighs
    They seek some safe retreat,
  Run here and there, they know not where,
    Till awful death they meet.

12. Their piercing cries salute the skies—
    Mercy is all their cry :
  " Our souls prepare God's grace to share,
    We instantly must die."

13. Some men yet found are flying round
    Sagacious to get clear ;
  In vain to fly, their foes too nigh !
    They front the flank and rear.

14. And now the foe hath won the day,
    Methinks their words are these :
  " Ye cursed, rebel. Yankee race,
    Will this your Congress please ?"

15. " Your pardons crave, you them shall have,
    Behold them in our hands ;
  We'll all agree to set you free,
    By dashing out your brains.

16. "And as for you, enlisted crew,
     We'll raise your honors higher :
     Pray turn your eye, where you must lie,
     In yonder burning fire."

17. Then naked in those flames they're cast,
     Too dreadful 'tis to tell,
     Where they must fry, and burn and die,
     While cursed Indians yell.

18. Nor son, nor sire, these tigers spare,—
     The youth, and hoary head,
     Were by those monsters murdered there,
     And numbered with the dead.

19. Methinks I hear some sprightly youth,
     His mournful state condole :
     "O, that my tender parents knew
     The anguish of my soul !

20. "But O ! there's none to save my life,
     Or heed my dreadful fear ;
     I see the tomahawk and knife,
     And the more glittering spear.

21. "When years ago, I dandled was
     Upon my parents' knees,

I little thought I should be brought
To feel such pangs as these.

22. " I hoped for many a joyful day,
I hoped for riches' store—
These golden dreams are fled away ;
I straight shall be no more.

23. " Farewell, fond mother ; late I was
Locked up in your embrace ;
Your heart would ache, and even break,
If you could know my case.

24. " Farewell, indulgent parents dear,
I must resign my breath ;
I now must die, and here must lie
In the cold arms of death.

25. " For O ! the fatal hour is come,
I see the bloody knife—
The Lord have mercy on my soul !"
And quick resigned his life.

26. A doleful theme ; yet, pensive muse,
Pursue the doleful theme :
It is no fancy to delude,
Nor transitory dream.

27. The Forty Fort was the resort
    For mother and for child,
  To save them from the cruel rage
    Of the fierce savage wild.

28. Now, when the news of this defeat
    Had sounded in our ears,
  You well may know our dreadful woe,
    And our foreboding fears.

29. A doleful sound is whispered round,
    The sun now hides his head ;
  The nightly gloom forebodes our doom,
    We all shall soon be dead.

30. How can we bear the dreadful spear,
    The tomahawk and knife ?
  And if we run, the awful gun
    Will rob us of our life.

31. But Heaven ! kind Heaven, propitious power !
    His hand we must adore ;
  He did assuage the savage rage,
    That they should kill no more.

32. The gloomy night now gone and past,
    The sun returns again,

The little birds from every bush
Seem to lament the slain.

33. With aching hearts and trembling hands
We walkèd here and there,
Till through the northern pines we saw
A flag approaching near.

34. Some men were chose to meet this flag,
Our colonel was the chief,
Who soon returned, and in his mouth
He brought an olive leaf.

35. This olive leaf was granted life,
But then we must no more
Pretend to fight with Britain's king,
Until the wars are o'er.

36. And now poor Westmoreland is lost,
Our forts are all resigned,
Our buildings they are all on fire—
What shelter can we find ?

37. They did agree in black and white,
If we'd lay down our arms,
That all who pleased might quietly
Remain upon their farms.

38. But O ! they've robbed us of our all,
    They've taken all but life,
    And we'll rejoice and bless the Lord,
    If this may end the strife.

39. And now I've told my mournful tale,
    I hope you'll all agree,
    To help our cause and break the jaws
    Of cruel tyranny.

"WARRIORS OF WYOMING.

"O! HAUGHTY was the hour,
    The hum, the brave array,
When sallied forth Wyoming's power,
    Upon the battle day.

"But soon, when hemmed by sudden foes,
    They gathered round to fight and die,
O! horrid was the shout that rose,
    And long and deep the dying cry.

"Fierce was the fight of strong despair,
    And fierce the savage yell,
And dreadful was the carnage where
    The warriors of Wyoming fell.

"No shouting of victorious pride
    Deceived the brave man's dying breath,
But murder raged on every side,
    And heavy blows, and blood and death.

"O, gloomy was the day,
    When the widowed mother heard

The roar of battle die away,
  And no returning band appeared.

" No more their burning hamlets gleam
    Along the narrow heath,
  Nor, stretching o'er the midnight stream,
    Reflect the fire of death.

" No more their little fort around,
    The warriors of Wyoming throng,
  They sleep beneath the frozen ground,
    Where the wind howls loud and long.

" And there the pausing traveller finds
    No grave-stone rising nigh,
  Where the tall grass bends, and the hollow winds
    May eddy round and sigh.

" O, when shall their silent home
    Its mournful glory gain !
  The volleyed roar and muffled drum,
    In honor of the warrior slain ?

" O, when shall rise, with chiselled head,
    The tall stone o'er their burial-place,
  Where the winds may sigh for the gallant dead,
    And the dry grass rustle round its base ?"

INDIAN ELOQUENCE.

A FEW suns more, and the Indian will live only in history. A few centuries, and that history will be colored with the mellow, romantic light in which Time robes the past, and, contrasted with the then present wealth and splendor of America, may seem so improbable, as to elicit from the historian a philosophic doubt of its authenticity. The period may even arrive, when the same uncertainty which hangs over the heroic days of every people may attend its records, and the stirring deeds of the battle-field and council-fire may be regarded as attractive fictions, or at the best as beautiful exaggerations.

This is but in the nature of things. Actions always lose their reality and distinctness in the perspective of ages ; time is their charnel-house. And no memorials are so likely to be lost or forgotten, as those of a conquered nation. Of the Angles and Saxons little more than a name has survived, and the Indian may meet no better fate. Even though our own history is so enveloped in theirs, it is somewhat to be feared that, from neglect, the valuable cover will be suffered to decay, and care be bestowed only on the more precious contents. "Be it so," exclaim some; "what pleasure or profit is to be derived from the remembrance? Let the wild legend be forgotten. They are but exhibitions of savage life, teeming with disgusting excess and brutal passion. They portray man in no interesting light, for, with every redeeming trait, there rises up some revolting characteristic in horrid contrast. Was he grateful?--So was his revenge bloody and eternal. Was he brave?—So was he treacherous. Was he generous?—So was he crafty and cruel."

But a more philosophic mind would say, "No! he presents a part of the panorama of humanity, and his extermination is an embodiment of a great principle— the same retreat of the children of the wilderness before the wave of civilization; hence arises a deep interest in his fortune, which should induce us to preserve, carefully and faithfully, the most trifling record of his greatness or his degradation." At a time when barbarous nations elsewhere had lost their primitive purity, we find him the only true child of nature—the best specimen of man in his native simplicity. We should remember him as a "study of human nature"— as an instance of a strange mixture of good and evil passions. We perceive in him fine emotions of feeling and delicacy, and unrestrained, systematic cruelty, grandeur of spirit and hypocritical cunning, genuine courage and fiendish treachery. He was like some beautiful spar, part of which is regular, clear, and sparkling, while a portion, impregnated with clay, is dark and forbidding.

But above all, as being an engrossing subject to an American, as coming to us the only relic of the literature of the aborigines, and the most perfect emblem of their character, their glory, and their intellect, we should dearly cherish the remains of their oratory. In these we see developed the motives which animated their actions, and the light and shadows of their very soul. The iron encasement of apparent apathy in which the savage had fortified himself, impenetrable at ordinary moments, is laid aside in the council-room. The genius of eloquence bursts the swathing-bands of custom, and the Indian stands forth accessible, natural, and legible. We commune with him, listen to his complaints, understand, appreciate, and even feel his injuries.

As Indian eloquence is a key to the character, so is it a noble monument of their literature. Oratory seldom finds a more auspicious field. A wild people, and region of thought, forbade feebleness ; uncultivated, but intelligent and sensitive, a purity of idea, chastely combined with energy of expression, ready fluency, and imagery now exquisitely delicate, now soaring to the sublime, all united to rival the efforts of any ancient or modern orator.*

What can be imagined more impressive, than a warrior rising in the council-room to address those who bore the same scarred marks of their title to fame and to chieftainship? The dignified stature—the easy repose of limbs—the graceful gesture, the dark speaking eye, excite equal admiration and expectation. We would anticipate eloquence from an Indian. He has animating remembrances—a poverty of language, which exacts rich and apposite metaphorical allusions, even for ordinary conversation—a mind which, like his body, has never been trammelled and mechanized by the formalities of society, and passions which, from the very outward restraint imposed upon them, burn more fiercely within. There is a mine of truth in the reply of Red Jacket, when called a warrior: "A *warrior!*" said he; "I am an *orator*—I was *born* an orator."

There are not many speeches remaining on record, but even in this small number there is such a rich yet varied vein of all the characteristics of true eloquence, that we even rise from their perusal with regret that so few have been preserved. No where can be found a poetic thought clothed in more captivating simplicity of

---

* An unqualified opinion to this effect has been expressed by JEFFERSON and CLINTON.

expression, than in the answer of Tecumseh to Governor Harrison, in the conference at Vincennes. It contains a high moral rebuke, and a sarcasm heightened in effect by an evident consciousness of loftiness above the reach of insult. At the close of his address, he found that no chair had been placed for him, a neglect which Governor Harrison ordered to be remedied as soon as discovered. Suspecting, perhaps, that it was more an affront than a mistake, with an air of dignity elevated almost to haughtiness, he declined the seat proffered, with the words, "Your father requests you to take a chair," and answered, as he calmly disposed himself on the ground: "My father? The sun is my father, and the earth is my mother. *I will repose upon her bosom.*"

As they excelled in the beautiful, so also they possessed a nice sense of the ridiculous. There is a clever strain of irony, united with the sharpest taunt, in the speech of Garangula to De la Barre, the Governor of Canada, when that crafty Frenchman met with his tribe in council, for the purpose of obtaining peace, and reparation for past injuries. The European, a faithful believer in the maxim, that "*En guerre, où la peau du lion ne peut suffire, il y faut coudre un lopin de celle du renard,*" attempted to overawe the savage by threats, which he well knew he had no power to execute. Garangula, who also was well aware of his weakness, replied, " Yonondio, you must have believed, when you left Quebec, that the sun had burnt up all the forests which render our country inaccessible to the French, or that the lakes had so overflowed their banks, that they had surrounded our castles, and that it was impossible for us to get out of them. Yes, surely, you must have dreamed so, and the *curiosity* of seeing so great a wonder has brought you so far. Hear, Yonondio : our *women* had taken their clubs ; our *children* and *old* men had carried their bows and arrows into the heart of your camp, if our *warriors* had not disarmed them, and kept them back when your messenger came to our castle." We cannot give a better idea of the effect of their harangues upon their own people, and at the same time a finer instance of their gratefulness when skilfully touched, than in the address to the Wallah-Wallahs by their young chief, the Morning Star. In consequence of the death of several of their tribe, killed in one of their predatory excursions against the whites, they had collected in a large body for the purpose of assailing them. The stern, uncompromising hostility with which they were animated may be imagined from the words they chanted on approaching to the attack : " Rest, brothers, rest ! You will be avenged. The tears of your widows will cease to flow when they behold the blood of your murderers, and, on seeing their scalps, your young

children shall sing and leap with joy. Rest, brothers,
in peace! Rest, we shall have blood!" The last
strains of the death-song had died away. The gleam-
ing eye, burning with the desire of revenge—the coun-
tenance, fierce even through an Indian's cloak—the
levelled gun, and poised arrow, forbade promise of
peace, and their superior force as little hope of successful resistance. At this moment of awful excitement,
a mounted troop burst in between them, and its leader
addressed his kindred : " Friends and relations ! Three
snows have only passed over our heads, since we were
a poor, miserable people. Our enemies were numerous
and powerful ; we were few and weak. Our hearts
were as the hearts of little children. We could not
fight like warriors, and were driven like deer about
the plains. When the thunders rolled, and the rains
poured, we had no place save the rocks, whereon we
could lay our heads. Is such the case now ? No!
We have regained possession of the land of our fathers,
in which they and their fathers' fathers lie buried : *our
hearts are great within us, and we are now a nation.*
Who has produced this change ? The white man !
And are we to treat him with ingratitude ? No ! *The
warrior of the strong arm and the great heart will never
rob a friend.*" The result was wonderful. There
was a complete revulsion of feeling. The angry
waves were quieted, and the savage, forgetting his

enmity, smoked the calumet with those whom the eloquence of the Morning Star alone had saved from his scalping-knife.

Fearlessness and success in battle were the highest titles to honor, and an accusation of cowardice was a deadly insult. A reproach of this kind to a celebrated chief received a chivalric reply. Kognethagecton, or, as he was more generally called, White-Eyes, at the time his nation was solicited to join in the war against the Americans, in our struggle for liberty, exerted his influence against hostile measures. His answer to the Senecas, who were in the British interest, and who, irritated by his obstinate adherence to peace, attempted to humble him, by reference to an old story of the Delawares being a conquered people, is a manly and dignified assertion of independence. It reminds one of the noble motto of the Frenchman : '*Je n'estime un autre plus grand que moi lorsque j'ai mon épée.*' "I know well," said he, " that you consider us a conquered nation—as women—as your inferiors. You have, say you, shortened our legs, and put petticoats on us. You say you have given us a hoe and a corn-pounder, and told us to plant and pound for *you—you men—you warriors.* But look at me—am I not full grown? And have I not a warrior's dress? Ay! *I am a man* —and these are the arms of a man—and that country is mine !" What a dauntless vindication of manhood, and what a nice perception of Indian character, is this appeal to their love of courage, and their admiration for a fine form, vigorous limbs, complete arms, and a proud demeanor! How effective and emphatic the conclusion, "all that country is mine!" exclaimed in a tone of mingled defiance and pride, and accompanied with a wave of the hand over the rich country bordering on the Alleghany!

This bold speech quelled for a time all opposition, but the desire to engage against the Americans, increased by the false reports of some wandering tories, finally became so vehement, that, as a last resort, he proposed to the tribe to wait ten days before commencing hostilities. Even this was about to be denied him, and the term traitor beginning to be whispered around, when he rose in council, and began an animated expostulation against their conduct. He depictured its inevitable consequences—the sure advance of the white man, and the ruin of his nation; and then, in a generous manner, disclaimed any interest or feelings separate from those of his friends; and added: "But if you *will* go out in this war, you shall not go without *me*. I have taken peace measures, it is true, with the view of saving my tribe from destruction. But if you think me in the wrong—if *you give more credit to runaway vagabonds than to your own friends—to a man—to a warrior—to a Delaware*—if you insist upon fighting the Americans—go! And I will go with you. *And I will not go like the bear-hunter, who sets his dogs upon the animal, to be beaten about with his paws, while he keeps himself at a safe distance.* No! I will lead you on. I will place myself in the front. I will fall with the first of you. You can do as you choose. But as for *me*, I will not survive my nation. I will not live to bewail the miserable destruction of a brave people, who deserved, as you do, a better fate!"

The allusion to their greater confidence in foreigners than in their own kindred is a fine specimen of censure, wonderfully strengthened by a beautiful climacteric arrangement. Commencing with a friend—and who so grateful as an Indian?—it passes to a man—and who so vain of his birthright as an Indian?—then to a warrior; and who more glorious to the savage than the man of battles?—and lastly to a Delaware—a word which rings through the hearts of his hearers, starts into life a host of proud associations, and, while it deepens their contempt for, the stranger and his falsehoods, imparts a grandeur to the orator, in whom the friend, the man, the warrior, the Delaware are personified.

The spirit of the conclusion added to its force. It was the outbursting of that firm determination never to forsake their customs and laws—that brotherhood of feeling which has ever inspired the action of the aborigines—a spirit which time has strengthened, insult hardened to obstinacy, and oppression rendered almost hereditary. It bespeaks a bold soul, resolved to die with the loss of its country's liberties.

We pass by the effect of this speech, by merely stating that it was successful, to notice a letter much of the same character as the close of the last, sent to General Clinch, by the chief who is now setting our troops at defiance in Florida. " You have arms," says he, " and so have we ; you have powder and lead, and so have we ; you have men, and so have we ; your men will fight, and so will ours, *till the last drop of the Seminole's blood has moistened the dust of his hunting-ground.*" This needs no comment. Intrepidity is its character.

View these evidences of attachment to the customs of their fathers, and of heroic resolution to leave their bones in the forests where they were born, and which were their inheritance, and then revert to their unavailing, hopeless resistance against the march of civilization ; and though we know it is the rightful, natural course of things, yet it is a hard heart which does not feel for their fate ; soon their graves will be all they shall retain of their once ample hunting-grounds. Their strength is wasted, their countless warriors dead, their forests laid low, and their burial-places upturned by the ploughshare. There was a time when the war-cry of a Powhattan, a Delaware, or an Abenaquis, struck terror to the heart of a pale-face: but now the Seminole is singing his last battle-song.

Some of the speeches of *Skenandoah*, a celebrated Oneida chief, contain the truest touches of natural eloquence. He lived to a great age; and, in his last oration in council, he opened with the following sublime and beautiful sentence: " Brothers—*I am an aged hemlock. The winds of a hundred winters have whistled through my branches, and I am dead at the top.*" Every reader, who has seen a tall hemlock, with a dry and leafless top surmounting its dark-green foliage, will feel the force of the simile. " I am dead at the top." His memory, and all the vigorous powers of youth, had departed forever.

Not less felicitous was the close of a speech made by *Pushmataha*, a venerable chief of a western tribe, at a council held, we believe, in Washington, many years since. In alluding to his extreme age, and to the probability that he might not even survive the journey back to his tribe, he said: " My children will walk through the forests, and the Great Spirit will whisper in the tree-tops, and the flowers will spring up in the trails—but Pushmataha will hear not—he will see the flowers no more. He will be gone. His people will know that he is dead. The news will come to their ears, *as the sound of the fall of a mighty oak in the stillness of the woods.*"

The most powerful tribes have been destroyed; and as Sadekanatie expressed it, "Strike at the root, and when the trunk shall be cut down, the branches shall fall of course." The trunk has fallen, the branches are slowly withering, and shortly the question "*Who is there to mourn for Logan?*" may be made of the whole race, and find not a sympathizing reply.

Their oratory, we think, *must* survive their fate. It contains many attributes of true eloquence. With a language too barren, and minds too free for the rules of rhetoric, they still attained a power of touching the feelings and a sublimity of style which rival the highest productions of their more cultivated enemies. Expression apt and pointed—language strong and figurative—comparisons rich and bold—descriptions correct and picturesque—and gesture energetic and graceful, were the most striking peculiarities of their oratory. The latter orations, accurate mirrors of their character, their bravery, immovable stoicism, and native grandeur, heightened as they are in impressiveness by the melancholy accompaniment of approaching extermination, will be as enduring as the swan-like music of Attic and Roman eloquence, which was the funeral song of the liberties of those republics.

At a Conference held at Wyoming, or Westmoreland, between Captain John in behalf of the Six Nations, and Colonel Butler of the Colony of Connecticut, Captain John said :—

" Brothers—We come to make you a visit, and let you know we were at the Treaty at Oswego, with Colonel Guy Johnson. We are all of one mind, we are friends, and bring good news.

" Brothers—We are also come to let you know, the Six Nations have been something afraid, but now are glad to see all things look like peace, and they think there will be no quarrel with each other, and you must not believe bad reports, or remember times that have been bad or unfriendly.

" Brothers—All our spirits are of one color ; why should we not be of one mind ? Continue to be brothers, as our fathers and grandfathers were.

" Brothers—We hope and desire you may hold what liberties and privileges you now enjoy.

" Brothers—We are sorry to hear two brothers are fighting with each other, and should be glad to hear the quarrel was peaceably settled. We choose not to interest ourselves on either side. The quarrel appears to be unnecessary. We do not well understand it. We are for peace.

" Brothers—When our young men come to hunt in your neighborhood, you must not imagine they come

to do mischief—they come to procure themselves provisions—also skins to purchase them clothing.

" Brothers—We desire that Wyoming may be a
place appointed where the great·men may meet, and
have a fire, which shall ever afterwards be called
Wyomick, when you shall judge best, to prevent any
jealousies or uneasy thoughts that may arise, and
thereby preserve our friendship.

" Brothers—You see but one of our chiefs. You
may be suspicious on that account, but we assure you,
this chief speaks in the name of the Six Nations. We
are of one mind.

" Brothers—What we say is not from the lips, but
from the heart. If any Indians of little note should
speak otherwise, you must pay no regard to them, but
observe what has been said and wrote by the chiefs,
which may be depended on.

" Brothers—We live at the head of these waters
(Susquehanna). Pay no regard to any reports that may
come up the stream or any other way, but look to the
head of the waters for truth, and we do now assure
you, as long as the waters run, so long you may depend
on our friendship. We are all of one mind, and we
are all for peace."

Perhaps we cannot present the reader with a greater
orator than GARANGULA ; or, as he was called by the
French, GRAND GUEULE, though Lahontan, who

knew him, wrote it Grangula. He was by nation an
Onondaga, and is brought to our notice by the manly
and magnanimous speech which he made to a French
general, who marched into the country of the Iroquois
to subdue them.

In the year 1684, *M. De la Barre*, Governor-General
of Canada, complained to the English at Albany, that
the Senecas were infringing upon their rights of trade
with some of the other more remote nations. Governor Dungan acquainted the Senecas with the charge
made by the French governor. They admitted the
fact, but justified their course, alleging that the French
supplied their enemies with arms and ammunition, with
whom they were then at war. About the same time,
the French governor raised an army of seventeen hundred men, and made other "mighty preparations"
for the final destruction of the Five Nations. But,
before he had progressed far in his great undertaking,
a mortal sickness broke out in his army, which
finally caused him to give over his expedition. In
the mean time, the Governor of New York was
ordered to lay no obstacles in the way of the French
expedition. Instead of regarding this order, which
was from his master, the Duke of York, he sent inter-
preters to the Five Nations to encourage them, with
offers to assist them.

De la Barre, in hopes to effect something by this

expensive undertaking, crossed Lake Ontario, and held a talk with such of the Five Nations as would meet him. To keep up the appearance of power, he made a high-toned speech to GRANGULA, in which he observed, that the nations had often infringed upon the peace; that he wished now for peace; but on the condition that they should make full satisfaction for all the injuries they had done the French, and for the future never to disturb them. That they, the Senecas, Cayugas, Onondagas, Oneidas, and Mohawks, had abused and robbed all their traders, and unless they gave satisfaction he should declare war. That they had conducted the English into their country to get away their trade heretofore, but the past he would overlook, if they would offend no more; yet, if ever the like should happen again, he had express orders from the king, his master, to declare war.

Grangula listened to these words, and many more in the like strain, with that contempt which a real knowledge of the situation of the French army and the rectitude of his own course were calculated to inspire; and after walking several times round the circle formed by his people and the French, addressing himself to the governor, seated in his elbow-chair, he began as follows :—

" *Yonnondio* [such was the general name for the French Governors of Canada], I honor you, and the

warriors that are with me likewise honor you. Your
interpreter has finished your speech. I now begin
mine. My words make haste to reach your ears.
Hearken to them.

" *Yonnondio.* You must have believed, when you
left Quebec, that the sun had burnt up all the forests,
which render our country inaccessible to the French,
or that the lakes had so far overflown the banks, that
they had surrounded our castles, and that it was impossible for us to get out of them ; yes, surely you
must have dreamt so, and the curiosity of seeing so
great a wonder has brought you so far. Now you are
undeceived, since that I, and the warriors here present,
are come to assure you that the Senecas, Cayugas,
Onondagas, Oneidas, and Mohawks are yet alive. I
thank you, in their name, for bringing back into their
country the calumet, which your predecessor received
from their hands. It was happy for you that you left
under ground that murdering hatchet that had been so
often dyed in the blood of the French.

" *Hear*, *Yonnondio*. I do not sleep ; I have my eyes
open ; and the sun, which enlightens me, discovered
to me a great captain at the head of a company of
soldiers, who speaks as if he were dreaming. He says,
that he only came to the lake to smoke on the great
calumet with the Onondagas. But Grangula says,
that he sees the contrary ; that it was to knock them

on the head, if sickness had not weakened the arms of the French.   I see *Yonnondio* raving in a camp of sick men, whose lives the Great Spirit has saved by inflicting this sickness on them.

" *Hear*, *Yonnondio*.   Our women had taken their clubs, our children and old men had carried their bows and arrows into the heart of your camp, if our warriors had not disarmed them, and kept them back, when your messenger *Akouossan* came to our castles.   It is done, and I have said it.

" *Hear*, *Yonnondio*.   We plundered none of the French but those that carried guns, powder, and balls to the Twightwies and Chictaghicks, because those arms might have cost us our lives.   Herein we follow the example of the Jesuits, who break all the kegs of rum brought to our castle, lest the drunken Indians should knock them on the head.   Our warriors have not beaver enough to pay for all those arms that they have taken, and our old men are not afraid of the war. This belt preserves my words.

" We carried the English into our lakes, to trade there with the Utawawas and Quatoghies, as the Adirondaks brought the French to our castles, to carry on a trade which the English say is theirs.   WE ARE BORN FREE.   WE NEITHER DEPEND ON YONNONDIO, NOR CORLEAR [the English].   WE MAY GO WHERE WE PLEASE, AND CARRY WITH US WHOM WE PLEASE, AND

BUY AND SELL WHAT WE PLEASE.* If your allies be your slaves, use them as such; command them to receive no other but your people. This belt preserves my words.

" We knocked the Twightwies and Chictaghicks on the head, because they had cut down the trees of peace, which were the limits of our country. They have hunted beaver on our lands. They have acted contrary to the customs of all Indians, for they left none of the beavers alive ; they killed both male and female. They brought the Satanas into their country, to take part with them, after they had concerted ill designs against us. We have done less than either the English or French that have usurped the lands of so many Indian nations, and chased them from their own country. This belt preserves my words.

" *Hear, Yonnondio.* What I say is the voice of all the Five Nations. Hear what they answer. Open your ears to what they speak. The Senecas, Cayugas, Onondagas, Oneidas, and Mohawks say, that when they buried the hatchet at Cadarackui in the presence of your predecessor, in the middle of the fort, they planted the tree of peace in the same place ; to be there carefully preserved, that, in the place of a retreat

---

* This proud declaration of Independence accords with and sustains the opinions expressed by us in our Indian narrative.

10

for soldiers, that fort might be a rendezvous for mer-
chants; that, in place of arms and ammunition of war,
beavers and merchandise should only enter there.

" *Hear*, *Yonnondio*. Take care for the future, that
so great a number of soldiers as appear there do not
choke the tree of peace planted in so small a fort. It
will be a great loss, if, after it had so easily taken root,
you should stop its growth, and prevent its covering
your country and ours with its branches. I assure you,
in the name of the Five Nations, that our warriors
shall dance to the calumet of peace under its leaves;
and shall remain quiet on their mats, and shall never
dig up the hatchet, till their brother *Yonnondio* or *Corlear*
shall either jointly or separately endeavor to attack the
country which the Great Spirit has given to our ancestors. This belt preserves my words, and this other,
the authority which the Five Nations have given me."

Then addressing himself to the interpreter, he said:
" Take courage. You have spirit; speak; explain
my words; forget nothing; tell all that your brethren
and friends say to *Yonnondio*, your governor, by the
mouth of *Grangula*, who loves you; and desires you to
accept of this present of beaver, and take part with me
in my feast, to which I invite you. This present of
beaver is sent to *Yonnondio*, on the part of the Five
Nations."

De la Barre was struck with surprise at the wisdom

of this chief, and equal chagrin at the plain refutation of his own. He immediately returned to Montreal, and thus finished this inglorious expedition of the French against the Five Nations.

Grangula was at this time a very old man, and from this valuable speech we became acquainted with him— a very Nestor of his nation—whose powers of mind would not suffer in comparison with those of a Roman or a more modern senator. He treated the French with great civility, and feasted them with the best his country would afford, on their departure.

Every one recollects the specimen of Indian elo- quence in the speech of Logan, a Mingo chief, to the Governor of Virginia.

In the spring of 1774, a robbery and murder were committed on an inhabitant of the frontiers of Vir- ginia, by two Indians of the Shawanee tribe. The neighboring whites, according to their custom, under- took to punish this outrage in a summary manner. Colonel Cresap, a man infamous for the many murders he had committed on those much injured people, col- lected a party and proceeded down the Kanaway in quest of vengeance ; unfortunately, a canoe with women and children, with one man only, was seen coming from the opposite shore, unarmed, and unsuspecting an attack from the whites. Cresap and his party concealed themselves on the bank of the river, and the moment the canoe reached the shore singled out their objects, and at one fire killed every person in it. This happened to be the family of Logan, who had long been distinguished as a friend to the whites. This unworthy return provoked his vengeance ; he accordingly signalized himself in the war which ensued. In the autumn of the same year a decisive battle was fought at the mouth of the Great Kanaway, in which the collected forces of the Shawanees, Mingoes, and Delawares were defeated by a detachment of the Virginian militia. The Indians sued for peace. Logan, however, disdained to be seen among the suppliants ; but, lest the sincerity of a treaty should be disturbed from which so distinguished a chief abstracted himself, he sent, by a messenger, the following speech, to be delivered to Lord Dunmore :—

" I appeal to any white man if ever he entered Logan's cabin hungry, and he gave him not to eat ; if ever he came cold and hungry, and he clothed him not. During the course of the last long and bloody war, Logan remained idle in his cabin, an advocate for peace. Such was my love for the whites, that my countrymen pointed as they passed, and said, Logan is the friend of the white men. I have even thought to have lived with you, but for the injuries of one man.

Colonel Cresap, the last spring, in cold blood, murdered all the relations of Logan, even my women and children.

"There runs not a drop of my blood in the veins of any living creature.—This called on me for revenge.—I have fought for it.—I have killed many.—I have fully glutted my vengeance.—For my country I rejoice at the beams of peace—but do not harbor a thought that mine is the joy of fear.—Logan never felt fear.—He will not turn on his heel to save his life. Who is there to mourn for Logan? not one!"

The speech of Sagnyn Whathah, *alias* Red Jacket, in reply to the address of a Missionary, at a Council of the Chiefs of " the Six Nations," in 1805:

Friend and Brother!

It was the will of the Great Spirit that we should meet together this day. He orders all things; and has given us a fine day for our council. He has taken his garment from before the sun, and caused it to shine with brightness upon us. Our eyes are opened that we see clearly; our ears are unstopped, that we have been able to hear distinctly the words you have spoken. For all these favors we thank the Great Spirit, and him only.

Brother! Listen to what we say. There was a

time when our forefathers owned this great island.
Their seats extended from the rising to the setting
sun: the Great Spirit had made it for the use of the
Indians. He had created the buffalo, the deer, and
other animals for food. He had made the bear and the
beaver; their skins served us for clothing. He had
scattered them over the country, and taught us how to
take them. He had caused the earth to produce corn
for bread. All this he had done for his red children,
because he loved them. If we had disputes about our
hunting-ground, they were generally settled without the
shedding of much blood. But an evil day came upon
us; your forefathers crossed the great waters, and
landed on this island: their numbers were small: they
found us friends, and not enemies. They told us they
had fled from their own country, through fear of wicked
men, and had come here to enjoy their religion. They
asked for a small seat; we took pity on them, and
granted their request: and they sat down amongst us.
We gave them corn and meat, and, in return, they gave
us *poison*. The white people having now found our
country, tidings were sent back, and more came
amongst us; yet we did not fear them. We took
them to be friends: they called us *brothers*, we
believed them, and gave them a larger seat. At length
their number so increased, that they wanted more land:
they wanted our country. Our eyes were opened, and

we became uneasy. Wars took place; Indians were hired to fight against Indians; and many of our people were destroyed. They also distributed liquor amongst us, which has slain thousands.

Brother! Once our seats were large, and yours were small. You have now become a great people, and we have scarcely a place left to spread our blankets. You have got our country, but, not satisfied, you want to force your religion upon us.

Brother! Continue to listen. You say you are sent to instruct us how to worship the Great Spirit agreeably to His mind, and that if we do not take hold of the religion which you teach, we shall be unhappy hereafter. How do we know this to be true? We understand that your religion is written in a book. If it was intended for us as well as you, why has not the Great Spirit given it to us; and not only to us, but why did he not give to our forefathers the knowledge of that book, with the means of rightly understanding it? We only know what you tell us about it, and having been so often deceived by the white people, how shall we believe what they say?

Brother! You say there is but one way to worship and serve the Great Spirit. If there is but one religion, why do you white people differ so much about it? Why not all agree, as you can all read the book?

Brother! We do not understand these things: we

are told that your religion was given to your forefathers, and has been handed down from father to son. We also have a religion which was given to *our* forefathers, and has been handed down to us: it teaches us *to be thankful for all favors received, to love each other, and to be united, we never quarrel about religion.*

Brother! The Great Spirit made us all; but he has made a great difference between his white and his red children:—he has given us different complexions and different customs. To you he has given the arts; to these he has not opened our eyes. Since he has made so great a difference between us in other things, why may he not have given us a different religion? The Great Spirit does right: he knows what is best for his children.

Brother! We do not want to destroy your religion, or to take it from you. We only want to enjoy our own.

Brother! We are told that you have been preaching to the white people in this place. These people are our neighbors. We will wait a little, and see what effect your preaching has had upon them. If we find it makes them honest, and less disposed to cheat Indians, we will then consider again of what you have said.

Brother! You have now heard our answer, and this is all we have to say at present. As we are about to part, we will come and take you by the hand : and we hope the Great Spirit will protect you on your journey, and return you safe to your friends.